Christmas Bite

Sharon Hamilton

Sharon Hamilton's Book List

SEAL BROTHERHOOD SERIES
Accidental SEAL Book 1
Fallen SEAL Legacy Book 2
SEAL Under Covers Book 3
SEAL The Deal Book 4
Cruisin' For A SEAL Book 5
SEAL My Destiny Book 6
SEAL of My Heart Book 7
Fredo's Dream Book 8
SEAL My Love Book 9
SEAL Encounter Prequel to Book 1
SEAL Endeavor Prequel to Book 2
Ultimate SEAL Collection Vol. 1 Books 1-4 /2 Prequels
Ultimate SEAL Collection Vol. 2 Books 5-7

BAD BOYS OF SEAL TEAM 3 SERIES
SEAL's Promise Book 1
SEAL My Home Book 2
SEAL's Code Book 3
Big Bad Boys Bundle Books 1-3

BAND OF BACHELORS SERIES
Lucas Book 1
Alex Book 2
Jake Book 3
Jake 2 Book 4
Big Band of Bachelors Bundle

BONE FROG BROTHERHOOD SERIES
New Year's SEAL Dream Book 1
SEALed At The Altar Book 2
SEALed Forever Book 3
SEAL's Rescue Book 4
SEALed Protection Book 5

SILVER SEALS SERIES
SEAL Love's Legacy

SLEEPER SEALS SERIES
Bachelor SEAL

STAND ALONE BOOKS & SERIES
SEAL's Goal: The Beautiful Game
Nashville SEAL: Jameson
True Blue SEALS Zak
Paradise: In Search of Love
Love Me Tender, Love You Hard

NOVELLAS
SEAL You In My Dreams Magnolias and Moonshine

PARANORMALS

GOLDEN VAMPIRES OF TUSCANY SERIES
Honeymoon Bite Book 1
Mortal Bite Book 2
Christmas Bite Book 3
Midnight Bite Book 4

THE GUARDIANS
Heavenly Lover Book 1
Underworld Lover Book 2
Underworld Queen Book 3

FALL FROM GRACE SERIES
Gideon: Heavenly Fall

NOVELLAS
SEAL Of Time Trident Legacy

All of Sharon's books are available on Audible,
narrated by the talented J.D. Hart.

About the Book

He is the eldest brother of three orphaned dark vampire waifs, bound by a lifetime vow of service to protect the offspring of the Golden Vampire Monteleone family. This is a debt that Lionel Jett can never discharge.

Phoebe Monteleone is a nineteen year old virgin, a Golden who has not taken the turning and who appears identical to her ancient great-great-grandmother, Maria Monteleone. Lionel Jett once harbored a secret and platonic love for Maria, who died as a mortal over three centuries ago.

The two vampire races are forbidden to mate, yet Phoebe and Lionel's attraction risks their very souls. In addition, the war brewing between the two species threatens the entire vampire society. When the two worlds collide, who will win out? Will their brief affair be worth an eternity of damnation? Or, can duty and honor leave room for love or the possibility of a happily ever after?

Chapter 1

LIONEL JETT HAD always thought Christmastime was more about angels, than celebrating vampires and their vampire society. But the emotional responses within his soul ticked like a timebomb. On the one hand, the beautiful candlelit services, held at night so he could attend, were striking and revived in him his higher calling to protect the innocent and all things good and pure. To eliminate evil.

Christmas celebrated the birth of an innocent, after all—a birth that would forever change humanity. Mortals believed that a woman conceived a child without having sex. Well, Lionel had seen many things in his three hundred years of life, and he couldn't rule out that this legend was actually fact. For if that occurred, then the possibility of redemption for himself, existed, as well as the chance for peace amongst the two vampire species.

His thick frame was forced to hunch a bit, his shoulders rounded so he could fit into the pews made for much smaller beings, mostly mortal. The wooden, hand-carved benches weren't constructed for huge, dark coven vampires, unless they were designed to say, "you are not welcome."

The Gregorian chants reverberated throughout the halls of the chapel where Marcus had first met his fated mate, Anne. Lionel watched a woman and her children light tiny, red votive candles in the alcove at the side. The light made their faces glow with that effect only mortals had. It was as if the goodness in them showed through their transparent skin, laced with the life-giving blood of their species, an elixir to some, and the highly prized substance others would die to protect.

Of all their traits, mortals' best gift to the world was that of love and innocence. Though some of their race claimed to be warriors, they would never be matches for the evil likes of the strongest dark covens.

But their God had told mortals they could achieve anything if they had faith. They had the gift of belief because their lives were so short. Of course, they believed in miracles. Unfortunately, they'd never live long enough to see true miracles or the way the world really was.

He could sign on to safeguard those ideas. It was something that spoke to him as a true warrior. He'd be able to defend those who had no clue they needed protecting. And he might die doing so, without any observance on their part.

Mortals were a strange combination of emotions and traits. They scared easily. They sometimes maintained bravado, like the David and Goliath story from their bible. They were underdogs, but like in the beloved story, they never stopped fighting though the odds were against them. They sometimes allowed anger to interrupt their lifeline or justified its benefits when it really never helped them.

But their most stunning quality was that of compassion. On that, they could teach the world. They had the gift of living a life untainted, if they so choose. Trusting in their God when, in actuality, their unseen vampire brethren were responsible for much of their safety. They believed in the laws of nature more than the laws of vampire. Lionel found this humorous.

The delicate children's choir made their way down the center aisle, each child holding an inverted paper cup with a white candle stuck into the base, so their little hands would be protected from any dripping wax. Their voices were soothing. He could make out every one of them, and it left him gentled, like listening to a babbling brook with water flowing over pebbles beneath the current. Each child had a distinctive series of tones, sometimes with thoughts laced in there, if the mind read was strong with them.

He remembered the night they said mass for Maria Monteleone, the only woman in Lionel's life he ever loved. He'd gladly foregone any chance at having a sexual relationship with her just to be in her presence and had begged her to live on after the death of her mortal husband, to take the turning late in her life. It was always a difficult decision for every Golden, all born as mortal children, and given the option to take the turning ceremony beyond after puberty. Most chose to live a life of immortality. But she, like her predeceased husband before her, refused, smiled, touched his cheek with her dainty lavender scented palm, and shared a tear with him.

"Lionel, my trusted protector, I know what's in your heart. I am given life enough with the knowledge that it's there. No need for us to speak of it or demonstrate it to anyone but ourselves. Our eternal secret."

He'd wanted to take her in his arms, but he would never shatter what they had. He was the only one she would take on as a protector, and the family knew Lionel would die doing so, if necessary. It was beautiful Maria who had saved his life by asking he and his two brothers be made vampire when she found all them left for dead after an attack by a dark coven lord who had obliterated their family.

The elder Monteleones had decided a trusted dark would do the turning, so that there would always be distance between Maria and her dear Lionel. He always wondered if she'd argued for another choice for him. Had she desired he be made in her own image or requested she be his maker? That question haunted Lionel for centuries.

He was there when she married Marcus and Paolo's father, was there as she bore him the dozen children, and as she continually turned down her husband's request to turn together. As a faithful husband, he dutifully remained at her side, mortal, sharing their short love and family.

Lionel was with her as her mortal life left her, on a starlit evening when the real stars were in her eyes, until they became fixed on him and then floated away. Like a piece of tissue paper, her spirit was gone, to become one with her God of Humans and her Mother Nature.

The hole in his heart was still the largest pain in his life. There wasn't a day that went by when he didn't wonder what would have happened if he'd chosen to take a more active role in that relationship with her or could have fought stronger for what he knew was something like an inter-species fating that never could be consummated.

He looked up at the bleeding figure of Christ nailed to a wooden cross, and he understood the man's pain, the regrets he might have had, his need to protect and love his flock, and to die for them. The miracle had been sent, only to have the evil factions of the mortal crowd kill him off. He walked amongst his people understanding this, all the while he remained on earth.

Lionel hoped that he still lived somewhere they called Heaven. For he and his vampire brothers and sisters, death was usually just the end of a long, long life. There was no Heaven. There was no happily ever after in the clouds that sent rain and wind and sometimes covered the sun and the moon. It was just death, with nothing beyond.

And yet, as he listened to the beautiful chanting and allowed the scents of mortals to envelop him, he felt the heat of their bodies, and some of their thoughts and worries. He'd like to pretend he believed in a time that would last, where everything would be perfect and not end. Where love, like the love he had for Maria, would reign eternal.

He was hopeful. It was a silly thought, but it was something that warmed him from the inside, as if he was a mortal again, as if he still held that innocent light inside.

THE WEDDING FEAST had begun. It was humorous that the Monteleones made a great show of eating to excess, though Lionel knew they'd be sick as dogs afterward. But they were stubborn about their secrecy, and as long as it was a mixed crowd of both trusted mortals and vampires of both species, the ruse would be continued. He stood with his arm around young Lucius while they watched his father, the handsome Paolo, and his new bride, Carabella, dance to the alluring viola music around a huge firepit stoked with logs the size of most humans. Paolo's face was filled with the mirth Lionel had always envied.

Out of the blue, Lucius asked his question. "Do you miss your brother?"

Jeb had traced the dark coven lord, Dag, to a desert somewhere on the other side of the globe, to end him, saving Lucius' father's life at the cost of his own.

"Of course, young prince. But his time had come. He'd had a wonderful and exciting life, keeping all you lot safe so your family can save the world. Don't you know that?"

Lucius thought about that for a short time. His six years was not commensurate with his knowledge of the ways of the world. He'd seen a lot in his brief time as son to one brother, only to find out he belonged to the other.

"Can I tell you something I've never told anyone?"

"Careful, young Lucius. I am bound to tell the truth, always."

"I know it. But I want to tell you anyway."

The boy's eyes followed his new stepmom and his father across the ampetheater. Lionel remembered days when there were dark coven sacrifices held in this space. He remembered the blood rituals of those difficult times, shortly before Maria's boys were grown. Although he was not sure, some of his relatives might have lost their lives in this very place. He shook off the vision and answered the boy. "You can certainly trust in my confidence."

"I don't miss my mother. I like that Cara is going to be my new mother. I think she'll bring me a little brother or sister."

Lionel was struck with this thought. Cara had been made, and the turning had taken place, which wasn't always successful, just before her mortal death. Paolo had given her his own blood. Even so, he wasn't sure Cara and Paolo could have offspring.

Lucius looked up at him. "Am I evil for saying this?"

Lionel knelt, placing his plate-sized hands on Lucius' forearms and elbows, his face eye-level with the boy. "You are very lucky, young princeling. Your mortal aunt was forgiven for your mother's demise because she protected all of you in that action. Maya would have not been the kind of mother you deserve. You deserve—"

He saw a group of young Goldens arrive, all of them in their teens and early twenties. Some had taken the turning, but several were clearly still mortal. He understood them to be friends since childhood.

As the group parted, some took to the dance floor. A tall dark-haired beauty swayed to the music, engaging the troupe of fiddlers who enjoyed her sultry dance moves. She was a curiously carefree mortal woman and Lionel couldn't take his eyes off her. She threw her head back, swung her hips from side to side and sent her light, peach-colored, mortal arms reaching out to the sky. She pulled up her long curls, holding them atop her head as she swiveled her hips and turned in his direction.

When their eyes met, her mouth dropped open and she became motionless, though the lively music continued behind her.

Lionel's heart leapt from his chest. Grateful she was not yet turned, he did not have to make some excuse if she heard the kettledrum in his chest that pumped his life force into overdrive. He resisted the urge to run to her, pick her up and carry her away, where he could satisfy all his questions.

Was this woman Maria, come back to life after three hundred years? The Maria he first knew before her marriage, her family, and her death?

The woman who stood across the bonfire from him looked identical to Maria.

Lucius wiggled free as Lionel had gripped his arms and gave his young charge welts.

"I'm sorry, son. I just thought I saw something. Forgive me if I hurt you."

Lucius remained two steps away from him, watching, as Lionel rose to full height, slowly uncoiling his enormous body. His mouth dry, his fangs aching, his mind reeled from the erotic thoughts that came at him like a firehose.

All too suddenly, she was gone. She'd pulled a brightly colored shawl over her head and neck and ran into the heavy foliage at the edge of the clearing.

Lucius turned to see what he was focusing on.

"The young woman who was dancing over there, she should not have gone into the forest alone. I fear for her life," he told his charge.

Lucius nodded. "Then go get her. Protect her, Lionel—or—" he peered up at him with a question on his face—"don't you want to?"

"It isn't that, but I'm to stay and protect you."

This part was true. He caught the attention of his younger brother, Hugh—"huge" as he was known to the ladies he bedded—and angled his head towards the woods. Hugh had a lapse in judgment and traced, instead of running like a mortal. Lionel scanned the crowd, and no one seemed to have noticed.

What am I looking for, brother? Hugh asked telepathically from behind the wooded surround.

"The spitting image of Maria Monteleone. Tell me it isn't so, brother. I pray to god she's safe, but I also pray it isn't her," he whispered.

"What?" asked Lucius.

"Sorry, I was giving instructions to Hugh."

Seconds later, a group of the young Goldens came screaming from the woods, followed by a dark vamp dressed in black rags. He stopped at the site of the campfire. His flesh peeled, and part of his face had been scratched off. His tongue hung limply, dripping bloody saliva.

The fiddle music stopped as several males from the partygoers came within feet of his disgusting frame. Several in the crowd began to moan, and there were a few suppressed screams. Precious seconds passed while the dark vamp and his would-be attackers held the standoff. Lionel scanned the young Goldens and didn't see any sign of the young Maria look-alike.

The dark vamp began to grin, his chest heaving. He fingered something around his neck Lionel had missed. It was the colorful shawl the young Golden had been wearing just moments before.

Lionel didn't have time to look for his brother. He traced to the creature, hoisting him high up into the sky and tearing his head from his body out of eyesight of the crowd below. He threw the remnants of the vamp's torso into another bonfire he found several miles away, at a distant farm. Before he let the body loose, he removed the shawl and stuffed it into his shirt.

Damages, brother? Are you there?

All is well, Lionel. She is alive, and safe. He was a rogue no coven to back him up. But it has us all shook.

He won't be back, Lionel told his brother.

He traced to the edge of the celebration, then walked through dense foliage toward the circle of fire. They had brought the young Golden toward the heat, and a group of elder men surrounded her, so he could not see her face. As he pressed himself towards the center, he could see the ugly, bloody bite on her neck and the rivulets of dark ooze descending down her chest, meeting between her breasts. Her eyes were dazed as she rolled her head back and cried.

Paolo was there, giving her first aid. Lionel sat next to her mother, who brought warm compresses and was whispering questions.

"Will she be infected, Paolo? She is still mortal and a virgin. Will this affect—?"

"No, Freya. She's intact. He didn't do a blood rape. She's intact."

"Oh, thank God," the woman sighed, leaning into Lionel's chest. Paolo gave him a frown.

"I have Lucius," said Hugh from the back of the crowd.

Freya's daughter stubbornly righted herself and accepted the salve that was applied to her neck taken from the kit Paolo carried with him 24/7. Her eyes swung around, perusing the crowd until she saw Lionel again, and their stares locked.

Her gaze lowered slightly, looking at something on Lionel's chest.

"He's gone, Madame," he told her. "He will no longer trouble you, or any of us."

But she was still peering at his chest. Looking down, he saw the remnants of her flowered shawl sticking out from the buttons on his white shirt. He drew it out, damp from the mixture of sweat and bloody detritus. He extended his arm and handed it to her.

She didn't look at the shawl. As she grabbed the cloth, her eyes were fixed on Lionel like he was her lifeline, her future.

He was instantly hit with the cold facts of their state. She would most likely be not his lifeline, but a straight ticket to Hell itself.

Chapter 2

PHOEBE WAS PLACED in the second seat of a Mercedes stretch limo for the trip back to her parents' villa. Paolo was with her. She was also being given an IV with her father's blood, for healing and strength. She'd heard the whispers over her near-sleeping body, about how her turning should be guarded and done soon to prevent another event like this one. It was felt she was now a target for the non-Golden covens. She should avoid tracing with her parents, turned siblings, or friends due to her condition. And no airline flights.

Since she was still pure and intact as a Golden virgin, it was thought her father's blood was best, but no one really knew the answers to these questions. Freya told them she'd have that talk with Phoebe. All of them were sure it would help making a turning easier, as she was now introduced to her father's Golden bloodlines. Acceptance of the new blood was always the trickiest part of the turning.

Her heart pounded fierce in her chest, and she felt

like her breath was sucking all the air out of the limo, then replacing it with her exhale. It was like a body sat on her chest. But upon opening her eyes, she noticed it was only the shawl, tucked up around her ears and under her chin. It gave her courage, for some strange reason, and hope. Her blouse had been removed earlier, she vaguely remembered, so that the shawl was against her bare, mortal flesh.

A healing vape came over her, not from the salve or the blood being administered, but from the shawl itself. She detected gentle steam pouring forth from it, coming directly toward her nose. She inhaled deeply, taking it all in. With the exhale, she felt her limbs go light, her head filled with twinkling stars that coursed throughout her body from her spine, around to her frontside, descending down to her toes.

One of the passengers had tried to remove the shawl, but she clutched it fiercely and stared into the eyes of her distant cousin, the kind and gentle Paolo. The man looked stunned.

She stumbled for words, but then finally came out with, "Please, sir, my modesty."

That took the tension off, and immediately the nervous banter continued. Paolo slipped little peeks between comments, carefully monitoring her expressions and answers.

Before they arrived at the villa, Paolo removed the IV infusion catheter with the life-enhancing blood from her father. "Hold this down hard for a few seconds," he said as he pressed a gauze pad to the puncture. Her fingers applied pressure until he found a wrap material that held the gauze in place, so it wouldn't bleed or form a bruise beneath the surface of her skin.

He checked her eyes, smelled her breath, which seemed odd, checked the sides of her face, her wrists, both ankles and declared she should be seen by the family physician as soon as possible, but that she was healthy and fully recovered.

As they pulled up to the villa, Paolo recommended, "She shouldn't leave the house until she's been checked out, however."

"Can she wash up?" Freya asked. "Or does she need—"

"No, she should wash the wound with soap. Then we'll apply more salve. You'll see when she removes the cloth she will have started to heal."

"Excellent. Thank you, Paolo," her father whispered.

While the men stayed downstairs, two household helpers and her mother brought her to her bedroom on the second floor, helping her to climb the enormous darkly carved bannister that switched back and forth to all three levels.

When they opened her door, the warm fire was already burning. Her bed was prepared and drawn back, and the room smelled of roses and lavender, her favorite fragrances. Everything was as she'd left it earlier in the day. Her hairbrushes were all angled the same direction on her dressing table. Her old baby crib filled with well-worn stuffed toys from her childhood stood in the shadows at the corner. Moonlight shone on the heavily polished wooden floor, giving off a blue cast to any smooth surface.

"Phoebe, we're going to undress you and then help you to the shower. Do you think you can stand and wash off, or do you need help?" her mother purred to her ear, making them both buzz. She heard extra inflections, sounds of her mother's voice in octaves she'd never heard before.

"I'm okay. I can—"

But they'd already removed her skirt, and placed it on a side chair, along with the shawl. Fully naked, she removed her sandals and stared into the full-length mirror on the way to her private bath. Her nipples were engorged and bright red, as if they'd been rubbed raw, and her face was flushed. But looking down at her sex, she noticed her lips were swollen and a deep rose-red in color. The sensation as she walked to the shower wasn't unpleasant.

"You must be sure to wash your neck with soap, little one," the maid whispered, then attached a clip to hold her curls up. The sound of the young woman's voice was like the wind blowing through the trees at the forest.

She was not left alone in the shower, but she kept her back to her audience, taking the soap and rubbing across her chest and up and around her neck, which was tender and swollen, around her chin and down her arms. As she smoothed the bubbles over her tummy and lower, her breathing hitched. She'd touched one side of her netherlips, and she was filled with such exquisite pleasure, she felt afraid she might pass out. She grabbed the shower wand and forced water between her legs and felt a tightening of muscles inside her lower abdomen she didn't know existed before.

She was handed an oversized bath sheet as she emerged from the shower, wrapping it tightly around her. Her mother lovingly applied more salve to her neck. She removed the clip and shook her hair loose, staring into the mirror.

Her eyes confirmed what her feelings were telling her: she'd stepped through a doorway. It had nothing to do with the dark coven vamp who tried to take her life, but the vamp who stood in the crowd and took her breath away. Something that was ancient and buried in her heart had risen from a bloody grave and was running loose inside her.

She was filled with terror.

She was also filled with erotic fantasies of pure pleasure.

She knew there was nothing she could do to stop it.

Phoebe slipped on a white gown and allowed her hair to be combed by her mother, who sent the others away.

"Phoebe, I know you heard some of what's been discussed between your father, Paolo, and I," Freya began.

"Yes, Mother."

"I want you to just put all that out of your mind right now. We'll get your evaluation done and see to it that everything is on a firm footing before we make any decisions."

Freya slipped around the stool to face her seated form. Her warm, lined face showed centuries of compassion. She tenderly held Phoebe's cheeks in the palms of her hands as she kissed her forehead and sighed.

"Your face is hot. Are you hot all over?" Her eyes bore into Phoebe and would not be denied.

"Yes, Mother." She worked to make her voice sound compliant, but her heartbeat had not slowed. She asked the question that had been lingering. "What is this sensation?"

"Your father's blood is strong in your veins. As a fully turned male vampire, even though he's your father, it's bound to affect you in special ways."

Phoebe wrinkled her nose and turned away from her.

"Nothing to worry about, Daughter." Freya touched her chin and turned her, so they could see each other straight on. "You are mortal, but not quite human. Do you understand this?"

She nodded yes.

"Your bloodline is sensitive to the vampire side of you. It seeks it as a natural protection, since it would be normal for you to seek a male vampire to protect you and help you bring young into this world who would be healthy. It is part of the selection process."

"But he's my father!"

"I'm talking about your yearning. Perhaps you have come into close proximity with another—someone who could bring you into the circle of fating. He may be distant, not even in this town, but he could be close by, perhaps."

"I would be that sensitive to it?"

Freya bowed her head and then smiled at her daughter. "It happens differently for different people. If it is beginning, it will be glorious. The most magnificent thing you've ever experienced in your life."

Her eyes twinkled with the extra moisture lingering there.

"This conversation has to remain confidential, just between the two of us, Mother. I don't think father would understand."

"Nonsense, Phoebe. Men don't understand many things about women, but they do understand the fating."

"But you need to promise me."

"All right. Now, come. Time for bed, Phoebe."

"How did it start for you?" Phoebe asked as she sat on the edge of the bed.

"I had to wait nearly two hundred years for your father. I used to worry that my early turning, before I'd found my mate, interfered with the sensors, or the fating, in some way. I thought I'd be barren, childless. And then when I met him, everything exploded onto the scene, and our romance was such a whirlwind. All those years and years of waiting were over in mere seconds it seemed. We got to work and right away got pregnant with you, then your three brothers."

"Yes, Mama. I've heard the stories."

"We never had any time to just become friends together, he and I. We had to live our lives completely different. We had to spend all our waking hours protecting all of you." She glanced out the window, biting her lower lip.

"And I'm grateful for all you've done."

"This is such a special time for you." She grabbed Phoebe's two hands in hers. "It will be confusing, but it will be worth it. Now, with all these coven leaders fighting each other, the beautiful parties, dances, balls, and galas are problematic. I wish you could have lived in those days. Now, we have to be so careful."

"Yes, Mama. I understand."

"So what I'm saying is that it might take a hundred years of protection, or more, until you find The One. This could be just a close encounter, a whiff of someone drifting by—someone you will meet years from now. We never know."

Phoebe wanted to tell her mother she had felt some kind of a shift but wasn't sure she should. Instead, she asked, "Will it be very obvious when it happens? Will everything shift in an instant?"

"Yes, my dear. But what I want to guard you most about is getting your hopes up too high. It doesn't mean anything if it takes a century or two or a few hours. You have to be sort of 'on call,' and yet that could last centuries. And still, you have to be ready, emotionally and physically, for when it comes."

"Yes, I understand."

Freya looked down at their entwined fingers. "But have you thought about the turning, Phoebe? How it might make things easier for—for all of us?"

It wasn't what she was expecting.

"You mean I could defend myself better, mother?"

"Yes. Partly that. But don't you have a feeling, a knowledge deep inside of what form you wish to take? Do you want to be a mortal woman or a Golden Vampire? I mean, one is weak, the other, well, stronger. Capable of protecting herself. Do you want to spend your life worried about the dark? About strange people and not being able to defend yourself?"

She nodded. She was going to tell the truth. "I've thought about it some, but not deeply. Mama, I'm unsure what form I want. I haven't made up my mind."

"If you turn now, by the time you find your mate, you will still be young and able to have children. If you take the turning at an older age, that comes with a different set of rules. Do you understand this? You risk the possibility of some injury or disfigurement to your body. Right now, dear Phoebe, your body is perfect. You have unsullied Golden bloodline in your veins. You'd remain this way forever."

"Yes, I see. And it would be more difficult to live alone, wouldn't it?"

"You want to leave the family?"

"I want to travel, Mother. I want to go to all sorts of places I've never seen. I'd like to live on the beach, in a cabin in the mountains, somewhere in the jungle—I want to explore so much."

"And you can do all that as a Golden. Your choices are so much more limited as a mortal. Not to mention how vulnerable you'd be."

"I know. But this is all I've known so far. I like who I am right now. Do mortals think about this? Worry about all this?"

Her mother chuckled, "All the time, my child. You know so little about them. Vain, doing all sorts of things to their bodies to cheat death. But luckily for their race, most of them are not like that. They accept that death is their partner. You, however, can control death. Send him elsewhere."

"Except I still will need protection when I have children."

"Yes. That's why we have the dark covens and others we hire to help with that. They live to take care of us, now, don't they?"

"Our protectors."

"Exactly."

"Like tonight."

"Well, yes. The dark security detail Paolo brought to watch over his son—he's the one who first noticed you and alerted others to get you to safety while he disposed of the garbage. He's a perfect example."

"So I would have a protector, like he is, then?"

"Yes."

"But what about one as a husband?"

Freya's head shot up, her eyes blazing. "Not as a *real* husband. Never that!" She softened a bit and then stroked the sides of her daughter's face. "Sweetheart, I can see I have not explained things to you properly. You can respect and even befriend them on a temporary basis before you are attached. But as far as a *life partner*, that is not allowed, my dear daughter. You will remain with your own kind, for the purity of the bloodline. We don't think a healthy child could ever come from such a union, even if it were possible, and the stories say it could never be."

"But what about Lucius?"

"He has no dark coven blood. Some witch and God knows other things, but no other coven blood. Paolo would never mate with a dark coven female." Then she added, "But Paolo was very lucky. His boy could have been deformed. We have seen some of these come into the world, recently. Horrible creatures."

She pulled the covers up.

"Come, you must rest. A good night's sleep will do you some good. Dream of a handsome Golden prince coming for you when you least expect it. It will be a glorious warm summer day, and you'll have flowers in your hair. You'll be partaking in the sacred ritual generations of Golden women have gone through. We don't wring our hands, complaining about our lives, our men, or our families. We embrace it with all the life and light we are given. It is our birthright, Phoebe. Yours too. Who knows? Perhaps you could have the double gift of having your fated mate turn you himself."

She hugged and kissed her, adjusting the cool sheets over her, touching her hair. As Phoebe lay back on the pillow and peered out at the stars from the open window, she watched her mother leave the room, closing the door behind her.

Then she remembered the shawl. Dashing out of bed, she searched the pile of clothes on the chair near the bathroom door and found it. She wrapped it around her neck and shoulders, dove back into the sheets and fingered the silky fabric as she watched the night sky again.

Her eyelids grew heavy. She heard music, saw bonfires and dancing maidens clutching maypole vines, lovers kissing in the shadows, and smelled cinnamon and other exotic spices, mixing with the strange vapor-like scent that refreshed her soul coming from the shawl.

She knew she was waiting. But for what? Her next adventure?

And with whom?

And would her family ever allow it?

Chapter 3

LIONEL PACED THE hallway outside the two-story walnut-paneled library at the great Monteleone estate. Hugh was at his side. He remembered how he'd paced the night Marcus and then Paolo came into the world, when Maria was in labor upstairs, screaming her lungs out. Half the men that night begged her husband to turn her during the birth to take the pain away from her mortal body, but she wouldn't have anything to do with it. Her husband defended her wishes.

It had been centuries since he'd felt so out of sorts, nervous. Filled with something he couldn't put his finger on. They'd both been summoned, *officially* summoned. He had a hard time wondering if, somehow, his employers sensed what was growing inside him, something he wished he could control and obliterate.

"I don't understand the summons, brother," Hugh whispered to him. "Is there anything wrong? Something I have missed?"

Lionel was pressing his fingernails into his own palms, barely listening to his brother.

"Yes," he began tentatively. "Something—but I can't make it out. I'm confused." He stared at his younger brother and shared the man's compassion.

"Not like you, Lionel. What confuses you? Or are they visions, signals from beyond—?"

Lionel clutched at the curly locks above his ears and pulled, as if the pain of nearly pulling them out by the roots would right his thinking. His heart was beating with adrenaline as if he'd been tracing all night long. He was filled with foreboding, and something else he couldn't identify.

Hugh tried to stop him, pulling his hands from his scalp. "Stop it, brother. You need a drink," he said, and he ran to the bar well-stocked with wines, elixirs, and spirits. Hugh poured a large tumbler for his brother and presented the crystal goblet to his lips. "Take it all down, Lionel. Calm yourself. Or do you want a meditation incantation? I can get one of the—"

"No! No witches. I've had it with witches."

Hugh accepted back the empty goblet thrust into his chest with a twinkle in his eye. "On the contrary, brother, when you need to forget everything, witches are exactly the right tonic for an overly developed and frustrated male of our species. You know this to be true."

"Not now. I have to keep my wits about me."

"But why?" Hugh replaced the liquid with more dark amber whisky, pouring a shot glass of Absinthe for himself. "Another. Together. Always together," he said as he handed the goblet back to Lionel.

"Always together," Lionel echoed and threw back the drink. He kept his eyes closed, searching his brain for something to focus on. Through the vague mist of the whiskey, he saw a huge bed with a woman sleeping there. He tried to study the environs but found it unfamiliar. He watched as her hands covered her breasts, rubbing flowery material over her ripe red nipples. He felt his tongue curl and his lips pucker as if he were suckling those nipples like juicy red cherries. The scent of her neck overwhelmed him as she turned and angled herself. His nose dove into the small hairs beneath and behind her pink ears. His wet lips drew across her cheek until they mated with her soft pillows, sucking them into submission. When she moaned into his mouth, he immediately opened his eyes in horror.

Phoebe! She feels me!

He worked to mask his errant thoughts just as he saw the back of Hugh's frame quickly turn to greet the crack in the library door as it opened to the warm, golden light inside.

"Hugh," acknowledged Marcus. His cousin's dark, kind eyes scanned Lionel's face. Out of centuries of instinct, Lionel lowered his and nodded to his master.

They were shown into the library, to a gathering of a handful of chairs in a semicircle, filled with Goldens of the Monteleone clan. Paolo carefully studied Lionel and Hugh as they were guided to chairs, completing the circle. The eyes continued to bore in, and Lionel worked a smile and nod to everyone else in the group, landing at last on Paolo's face.

"Sir."

The gesture was returned with formality.

Marcus began the discussion after a male servant brought a silver tray of spirits into the room, including two chilled glasses of blood for those who needed nourishment. Lionel took one of those and noticed the effects of pure Golden elixir as it coursed throughout his bloodstream. His stomach stopped churning, but his heartbeat remained rapid, though no longer labored.

"This meeting is called in an effort to discuss measures that are deemed urgent and necessary." Marcus remained standing and touched Lionel's shoulder. "These two brothers are a part of this family in every way but one. And if I could change that, I would."

Lionel darted a look to his employer.

"Yes, you're surprised at this, old friend?"

"I am," Lionel said with gravel in his throat nearly cutting off his wind. Marcus had never called him "old friend" before.

Lionel searched Hugh's face and got a reactive shrug.

"The brothers have sacrificed much—their own brother, in fact—to protect this family. They have spilled their dark blood to save ours. I trust them more than members of my own family," Marcus continued.

Lionel watched Paolo squirm. His son, Lucius, was the offspring of a union between he and a Golden part-witch female, luckily now dead. But Maya's family was a constant sore subject in the Monteleone discussions of bloodlines and family. His brother, Jeb, had given his life for this mixed-race boy and his father.

"Paolo and I have some things to share with you. But I must first tell all of you, this meeting is being done in complete secrecy. No others outside our immediate family are to hear what I have to tell you. And if anyone repeats any of this to persons—no matter who they are—outside this room, it is not only grounds for dismissal from this little council. It would mean your own death."

Several of the men shifted themselves. Someone swore in Italian. Paolo stared at his boots, his shoulders hanging down limply at his sides as he took a huge sigh. Whatever it was had been weighing on both of them heavily.

Marcus went to the library shelves and drew out a book. "This, gentlemen, is the missing book to my grandfather's collection." He placed the book on a table at the edge of the circle. "It is the history of our family. There are many things in here that give us clues to what is going on right now between the two vampire covens."

Marcus studied his brother and then continued.

"It refers to another book, The Book of Spawn, which we have yet to find." He glanced again at Paolo, who nodded in agreement.

"But we are doing ongoing research. We'll find it, eventually," said Paolo, making eye contact with the rest of his family. He gave quick nods to Hugh and Lionel and then looked back down at his boots.

"Yes, Paolo's Carabella is the one who discovered this book." Marcus pointed to the family tome. "She's since turned it over to us so that the library is complete and under guard."

"This is information we're allowed to read?" said one of the members of the group.

"As a Monteleone, yes. No other Golden is allowed," answered Marcus, gruffly. "And you are commanded not to discuss it with any of your wives, your offspring, your parents, or other relatives. No one outside of this room will be allowed access to these books, or to this library as of tonight."

"So why is all this being shared, and why with them?" one of the other members asked, pointing to the two Jett brothers.

"Because their trust and loyalty are without question," whispered Marcus. "They are mistaken as outsiders to some of our family, but mostly to the dark hordes with whom they share a bloodline, and I'm choosing to leave it that way, for now. We are going to need their access to some of the other coven leaders, any of the ones who are not at war with the Monteleones."

"But won't their loyalties lie with the dark covens?" asked an aging member of the audience. His worried brow was duplicated by several of the other elders present.

"Yes, how can you be sure, Marcus?" added one of the others. "And hear me, no offense intended, Hugh and Lionel. I mean you no disrespect, but our rules are based on natural selection. *Our* blood never lies. But, there are things beyond even *our* control," the other elder continued. "How would they be expected to share this to those of us outside their species?"

Marcus seemed unfazed. "I have asked myself this question, and I have looked inside their hearts. I see only loyalty and service there." Marcus gripped Lionel's shoulder again, squeezing it to the point of pain.

Lionel remained motionless, like a rock, envisioning slugs and cold slimy things in the earth so as to mask any emotions or fears. He understood the questions about his loyalty, but it didn't set well with him.

"You think this is just against the Monteleones?" asked Hugh, breaking the awkward silence.

"Gentlemen," Marcus began, "We think it's coordinated to take us out first. Then they'll work on some of the other families, who have allowed others infiltrating their bloodlines. For some reason, our fated lines have remained nearly pure." He glanced quickly at Paolo, who winced but didn't look back at his brother.

Lionel's stomach began to gurgle, which started Hugh in a chuckle that soon spread to all the other members.

"Apparently, my wife's blood cocktail doesn't agree with you," Marcus said with a smirk.

"Pardon me, but no. That's not it. That could never be it." Lionel snuck short glances at several of the other members to make sure his point was made. Hugh continued to chuckle until Lionel hit him on the bicep and nearly toppled the huge vamp.

"Okay. It's late, and we're tired. There will be more coming, which will mean more meetings. But not tonight. It's been a big weekend and the young bride and groom are safely on their way sailing around the world. The party was saved by the heroics of these two." Marcus grabbed Lionel's shoulder again and held it like the top of a staff. The rest of the room clapped. "So now it's time for some of us to travel, some of us to visit and vacation, and some of us to go back to bed."

Everyone stood in a circle, arms around each other's shoulders. Paolo led the circle chant, which everyone said in unison. Lionel had learned it many decades ago, but had never been part of the circle, until this evening.

"We are one family, one people, one blood. We eternally stand for what is precious and good, what is innocent and pure. We pass the flame of eternal life on to the worthy."

THE CONCLAVE BROKE. Both Jett brothers shook hands with most the other members and took their exit. Lionel felt the eyes of the two Monteleone brothers on his back as he and Hugh walked across the crushed granite driveway to their motorcycles.

"You game for some recreation, brother?" Hugh asked. It meant he wanted to share a female. The need for blood was equally as important as his lust for sex.

"No, Huge. I don't trust myself tonight." He stared up at the moon, remarking how many stars were out tonight in the clear midnight sky. The other Monteleones left, piling into two vehicles. The orange square of the front door closed, and the brothers were alone at last under the dome of nature, staring up through old gnarled olive trees.

"Trust yourself? Your mood is curious tonight, Lionel. Where is your mind?"

"As I mentioned, all these changes, even tonight's meeting, has me uneasy. For some reason, I'm feeling the need to remain vigilant. It's like there's a fight about to break out any second. Don't you feel it?"

Hugh shrugged, turning with is arms outstretched as if willing all the dark forces of the universe to hit him square in the solar plexus. "I feel nothing, except a need to feed and spawn."

"Nights like this I miss Jeb," Lionel whispered to the moon.

Something rustling in the bushes made them both jump. A huge dark cat ran across the driveway and scampered around the stone foundation of the enormous villa.

"I thought I heard him yesterday," Hugh sighed. "Even smelled those disgusting little things he liked to suck on."

"Sardines." It made Lionel begin a rumbling chuckle that soon was uncontrollable.

"Yuck." Hugh shook his head and shoulders in a shiver of movement. "What was it about them he liked?"

"The salt. He had a salt tooth."

"I could never understand—" Hugh began.

Still smiling, Lionel jumped on his kick starter and allowed his motorcycle to roar to life. He looked behind him as Hugh did the same.

The two brothers followed the road which bordered the river, using moonlight and their preternatural vision to guide them. Night creatures cavorted in the woods and fields as they passed. Owls swung low searching for prey. Several families of tree bats hovered above the water's edge. Lionel loved the simplicity of nighttime. Movements were efficient, intentional, with life or death consequences. All creatures of the night hunted.

At last, they came upon their bungalow, buried behind rows of thick berry vines. Nestled amongst the vines was an automatic gate behind a well-traveled path just wide enough to allow them and their bikes through. Lionel swished over the tire tracks outside with a broken oak tree branch full of dead leaves to hide their entrance to mortal interference.

Inside, the little home was cozy and warm. Their part-time daytime staff, hired by Marcus himself, had long since retired, but left behind a roaring fire and a hearty beef stew simmering on the stove they would dispose of when they retired for their daytime sleep. The windows had been shuttered and draped over. Each brother retired to his own bedroom, leaving Jeb's room door wide open, but paying respects to him first before retiring. A red candle was lit beside Jeb's bed, as if to leave a light on for his safe return, which would never occur.

Lionel locked his door and placed the iron key beneath his pillow. He wished he could sleep with the windows open, so he could watch the stars all night until the sky pinkened like the bottom of a cherub, but that was too dangerous in these times. He'd awaken to save himself from the dawn, but it was the other night creatures, the other dark coven members he feared most. Safety precautions were taken with the perimeter walls.

Removing all his clothes, he decided to sleep naked. The clean white sheets felt like a mortal woman's backside tonight as he snuggled to find a comfortable position. He knew it might take him a few hours to drop off. He placed his arms beneath his pillow, rested his head, and waited, thinking.

He too had picked up a sensation of Jeb, but not in the same way Hugh had. His aura traveled on a dry wind from the south. He'd been in the old Souks in Marrakesh and Casablanca, where they sold colorful spices in huge reed jars as tall as a man and oils infused with every kind of scent imaginable. He wondered if his strong sense of smell was picking up something from across the Mediterranean, something from North Africa. But he felt Jeb was calling to him in a message from that parched, scented wind.

He traced the roughhewn timbers that held his ceiling in place, noticing the lattice pattern and circular indentations of a skilled artisan's blade. His eyelids felt heavy, and he let them fall.

He drifted off to a gentle sleep, hearing sounds of the ocean lap upon a sandy shore, but as he became more discerning, he determined the rhythm of the sea was really the sounds of heavy breathing. He was back in the room with the golden fireplace illuminating the mounds and valleys of the mortal woman's body.

He knew he could turn her over with a suggestion she'd not recall but was afraid to try at first and then gave in to the urge to see her writhing in her bed. Her shoulder turned, then came her arm, and, at last her torso lay back into the bed, as her hands pushed back the covers. Her body had produced delicate beads of sweat like tiny diamonds that shimmered in the light of the flames. Around her neck was draped the shawl that he'd held inside his shirt as he traveled to her, his heart ardently striking its dull cord like a homing beacon.

He dared not speak her name, or even think it. She was agitated, flailing back and forth, eventually turning back to her stomach. One thigh and butt cheek were exposed to the flickering light in the otherwise silent room. He could almost feel the firm flesh beneath his fingertips as he smoothed over her, searched for the crevice between her cheeks. His mouth watered.

I can taste you, Phoebe.

He'd said it in his mind before he could stop himself. He should open his eyes and begin reading a book, or watching some television, but he couldn't stop the dream.

She rotated her body again, laying on her back and pushing the covers down over her chest. It moved beyond her waist, and she raised her nightgown and then exposed the juncture between her legs. With her chin extended toward the ceiling, she raised her knees, touched herself with one hand, and whispered, "Taste me."

Lionel sat up immediately. He scrambled to his feet, examining the bed as if it was to blame for his erotic thoughts, and then noticed his hard-on. He swore, storming off to the shower, and stood beneath the cold spring water spray until his teeth began to chatter. He lathered his body with the heavy clove and cinnamon-scented soap he'd bought in the village. He rinsed his mouth out, even adding soap to his tongue to interfere with the pheromones he'd inhaled in his dream.

Exhausted, he sat dripping wet, shivering in the dark room, alone. He couldn't afford to sleep until he was sure the vision he'd had was completely severed from his psyche.

Minutes turned into three hours. He allowed the cold to chill his soul even as he heard sounds from the outside that indicated dawn was approaching. Any hint of emotion or warmth, he stomped out until sleep began to overtake him.

He stumbled to his cold bed, wishing for oblivion, death. Seeking a grave somewhere. Dirt. Worms, stones, and carcasses of dead animals. Bones staring back at him. Just before he plunged deep into the midnight sea of sleep that was his legacy, he heard her once more.

"Taste me."

Chapter 4

PHOEBE WAS STARTLED when her attendant awakened her. Her gown was twisted about her waist and upper chest, the covers nearly ripped from her bed.

"Goodness, Princess, you've had an awful night," Selena said to her charge.

Phoebe went back into her memory and couldn't recall anything, except the warm glow deep inside her soul. She'd been drifting in an erotic wind where fabric, and coarse skin of a mysterious male's cheek pressed against her breasts and made her rise up to present herself. It was unlike anything she'd ever felt before.

"Is there anyone else in the household?" she asked.

"No, miss. Your mother and father are downstairs in the garden room. But they are expecting visitors this morning. They asked me to get you ready to receive them."

"Who?" Phoebe asked.

"Don't know, sweet child. A delegation of some kind, I think."

Just then, they heard an automobile pull up to the front. They both watched as an elderly priest extracted himself from the back seat then placed his cap firmly atop his bald head. With the help of an accolade and two other younger priests in black robes, he was ushered to the entrance of the villa.

"Come, Phoebe, we must prepare quickly. Your mother will be angry with me if we don't get down there soon."

"I'm starving," Phoebe moaned, holding her stomach.

"She's prepared a full breakfast for our visitors, it seems. Can't you smell it?"

She could. Satisfied with the clothes laid out, she sent Selena away to announce her imminent arrival. She jumped into the shower, again feeling the sensitive and blooming parts of her body. Fear had left her. Her mood turned happy now that the effects of the bite and the dreams it had caused last night were distanced.

She did her hair up in a bright red ribbon and wore the deep red garnet necklace her mother had given her last year, with the matching heart-shaped earrings that had belonged to her distant great-grandmother. She wore a dark burgundy frock over flowing black leggings, slipped on her black leather pumps, and examined herself in the mirror after applying red lipstick.

The raw marks on her neck were still present, but the healing had nearly completed. The remaining tissue was swollen and as bright red as her lips. She used some of the salve left behind, dabbing the green substance over her scarring flesh, and noticed how it made her surface skin tingle then numb.

Not knowing who her visitors were, she decided it would be prudent to drape a clean shawl around her shoulders to cover up the mark, in case the event wasn't known to the audience downstairs. Taking the ends of the material and tossing them behind her, she straightened her bedding, and skipped her way downstairs to the waiting crowd.

Father Domenico Flavius regarded her from his sitting position in the garden room like a cherub. His round face and pink shiny cheeks resembled a baby's bottom.

"Ah, Freya, how lovely she has grown!" He set his plate of sweets down and stood, outstretching his arms. "Child of God in Heaven! The Lord looks down upon you with favor!"

She ran toward him, remembering him from her brother's birthday party some years ago when he took a vow as a youngster to help in the church—a vow which was quickly expunged by the family. Her brother was a kind and helpful soul who wished to live a life of service to his community.

"Brother Domenico! I'm surprised you remember me. I have all my teeth at last! See?" She gave him a wide smile showing her mouthful of perfect white teeth. Then she hugged the rotund gentleman. She noticed the black-robed younger priests fidget, switching their weight from leg to leg while they presented brittle smiles. Her father was frowning but her mother clasped her hands together and beamed.

"Look at you, my dear," Father Domenico said as he held her at arm's length. "As beautiful as your mother, as all the women of your family." His hand cupped her cheek.

Phoebe felt her cheeks blush from all the attention. She recognized one of the young priests.

"Mario! You've taken the cloth."

"I have, dear Phoebe. Although looking at you now, I'm seriously reconsidering that option. Was I premature?" he said as he winked at her. His stiff blond-colored hair appeared not to have been combed for several days and stood out at his sides like straw.

Phoebe had played with Mario and his brothers all during her childhood, until his parents intervened over two years ago as Phoebe blossomed from child to young woman. It was explained that it would be improper for her to be alone with him, unless accompanied by members of her family and the security detail employed to watch over the children.

"You have a good heart, like Damian."

Phoebe's mother put her palm to her mouth at the mention of Phoebe's brother, who was away at a camp for the young Goldens going into family winery businesses.

Mario glanced at Father Domenico nervously and then gave Phoebe a chaste kiss on her cheek. "Bless you, Phoebe. You always see the good in everyone. That's a gift," he whispered, with his eyes downturned.

Her father cleared his throat and extended his arm around Father Domenico. "Phoebe, your mother and I are making plans for your coming of age party."

His smile was plastered to his face, but his eyes were deadly serious. Phoebe knew well there was another meaning to them. Her mood darkened at the reminder of the decisions she was being pressured to make. But it was awkward to discuss it with members of the clergy, as well as childhood friends, who were all mortal, with no vampiric bloodlines. It felt like a betrayal of her friends that they were excluded.

"Yes, Father. That would be lovely." She worked to make her voice sound compliant, as she always did around him. But she clearly saw the strain in his face, the wrinkle between his eyes he could not mask. And her mother had stopped smiling.

Even the older priest seemed a bit ill at ease.

"Is there a special someone who could also be part of this celebration, my dear family?"

He looked from Salvatore Dominichelli, to his wife, Freya, and then back to Phoebe without getting a nod or answer of any kind. His fingers started flickering beneath his robes, which extended past his first two knuckles.

At last Phoebe burst out into laughter to break the tension. "Father! You rascal! Of course not. I'm way too young."

Her mother angled her head and sweetly smiled. Her father ground his teeth and held his jaw firm.

She twirled, her eyes dancing over all the faces in her presence. She hugged herself, pulling the shawl tight across her chest for comfort. She didn't want to show the bite mark. The older priest would certainly be able to recognize it. Nor did she want to show the goosebumps on her arms and chest. She sashayed towards the kitchen fireplace, hugging their cook along the way.

"I'm starved! Can I join you in breakfast?" she finally asked the nonplussed crowd.

"Yes, yes. Forgive me, Father. Where are my manners?" Freya said as she flitted over to the kitchen, lifting trays of breakfast breads, jams, and several fancy egg dishes.

Phoebe sank into the chair at the head of the table without waiting for anyone else to join her and dove into the food. It was a welcome distraction.

AFTER THE ENTOURAGE left, Phoebe turned from the closed front door and addressed her parents.

"And what was *that*?"

"Phoebe, you remember—?" Her mother began.

"It's been decided you need to either take seriously your choices or take a husband. Your mother and I are beside ourselves with worry, now that you've come to the attention of the dark covens."

"That might not be true," Phoebe protested.

"Oh, for Heaven's sake, Phoebe, look around you," her mother added. "You have to be able to feel all this change going on. Your father and I do. You told me last night—"

"In confidence, Mother. Does half the village know about all this, this decision made without consulting me?"

"No final decision has been made, Daughter," her mother whispered, then searched her husband's face for help.

Her father stepped closer and took both her hands in his. "You must know how much I love you, Phoebe. I just wouldn't be able to live with myself if anything happened. I could drop everything else and guard you every waking minute myself, but that's not realistic. We are worried. And we don't think history is lining up very favorably for our family, for any of the Golden families. Even the Monteleones are worried."

"I'm sorry, Father." She searched his face, noticing his lack of aging, the familiar lines that remained ever since she was old enough to remember him. The older she got, the closer in physical age to both he and her mother she was becoming. She knew the mortal population would notice it sooner or later. It meant that some children who elected not to turn had to leave their homes to live elsewhere.

He drew his large arms around her and kissed the top of her head. "Phoebe, I'm not sure why I am so protective of you. You are smart, capable, and beautiful. You've been a wonderful, obedient daughter, accepting of all that is about this family. Not rebellious like some of the other families. You are a model for all young Golden virgins. A father couldn't ask for anything more."

His hand rested at the back of her head and lazily rubbed her curls. The heat from his body felt reassuring to her, even though there was going to be a large "but" in his conversation soon.

She decided to take a chance he might understand her. "I honestly haven't decided, Father," she said to his chest.

"Could you—?" His breath hitched as the emotions overtook the normally cool and logical family icon. "Could you consider speeding up your choice? Or could it be possible you could take a husband, even if he wasn't fated to be yours? Not a mate, but a protector."

She withdrew from him, scanning their faces back and forth.

"A marriage without love? Just a protection? That would be a lie."

"An arrangement," said her mother.

"But I thought you said—"

"Your father and I have discussed it at length after we spoke. It would be *with* the understanding when the fating came, you'd be free to go. That you'd remain unsullied, a virgin, until that time."

"But you said this was never allowed."

"In special circumstances," said her father.

"With a non-Golden husband? A protector?"

Both her parents nodded. "It's allowed and done. Especially now that these wars are beginning, Phoebe.

We are having to resort to desperate ways to protect our young. You are the future of this family. You and your siblings," said Dominichelli.

"How would this be arranged?"

"We would pair you with someone we *trust*. You'd have no obligation. In fact, you'd be requested *not* to consummate the marriage. It wouldn't be a *real* marriage. But it will protect your place in our bloodline. And your womanhood."

"But who?"

Chapter 5

THE MESSAGE STARTED as a shrill whistle, coming from the south. Lionel had been polishing an old knife his grandfather had given him when he was a boy of not more than ten. He'd been waiting until Hugh rose from his slumber.

As he angled his head, the whistle became louder. He shook his head and then tapped his ears as if to allow bugs to fall from his brain. Nothing stopped the noise.

Hugh swung open his door and stood naked, holding an axe.

"Hold there, brother. I mean you no harm," shouted Lionel.

"One thing to be rousted up from a wonderful wet dream and quite another to hear a banshee—it is from a creature, not a man-made instrument," Hugh spat. "The bastard who dares do this will pay for it by giving me his dick."

"What if that whistle is a woman?"

Hugh tossed his head from side to side. "Damn! It's incessant. I hope she's an ugly witch or she-banshee, a female troll with warts and green skin. Would be a shame to behead a beauty, now, wouldn't it?"

The sound stopped abruptly. The two brothers waited several seconds before relaxing. Lionel spat on the metal blade he was polishing, rubbing it against the sharpening stone by candlelight. Hugh laid the axe into the doorway and removed blood from the refrigerator, adding it to a protein shaker and topping it off with whiskey. After giving the mixture several vigorous shakes, he drank the contents down and let out a gut-wrenching burp.

"You'll never marry, Hugh. I think that alone could undo any fating coming your way."

"Nah, I don't believe in it any longer. It would have happened by now, with all the sampling we've done."

"We've been tethered to one family, one employer. We've not traveled much for the past century. Who knows what's out there?" Lionel had pondered it for decades.

Hugh rinsed his shaker. "You want me to make a concoction for you, Brother?"

"Nope. I'm not hungry at the moment."

Hugh collapsed into the heavy wooden chair and sat across the table from Lionel's finishing cloths, oils and polishing pastes. "You seem calmer today. You thinking more clearly?"

He nodded. "I am. I'm of a good frame of mind tonight. My rest was restorative. You?"

Hugh got up and suddenly discovered he was still naked. "Now I'm the one distracted. But, unlike you, I'm going to go hunting. I can see you won't join me."

Lionel's cell rang. Both brothers noted the screen read *Marcus M.*

"Sir?" he answered.

"I have some news you'll want to hear. Jeb has been found. Alive."

Lionel stood. Even Hugh had heard the scratchy voice of their employer from the cell phone and scrambled to his feet, tracing through the table to put his ear against the little device.

"H-How is that possible?" Lionel asked. His heart was racing. He'd hoped the signals were not just his over-active imagination.

"He was rescued by a Bedouin tribe in the Sahara, near death. He was clutching to the charred, dead remains of Dag, who is confirmed truly dead. Good and dead, thank God."

Lionel was almost giddy. It had always struck him so odd that Goldens liked to swear and thank God for things he had nothing to do with, if he even existed.

"Where is he?" Hugh blurted out.

Marcus chuckled. "Right now, he's wrapped like a mummy in a very thick carpet, and stored in a cool, dark place, so that he doesn't lose any more flesh before he can regenerate."

"He needs a host. Are they feeding him, Sir?" Lionel asked.

"Apparently, they know all about your kind. And they recognized the vamp who perished at his hands, which is why he was spared, I'm told. Dag was an enemy of those people."

"So they are a dark coven, then?" Lionel asked.

"I don't think so. In fact, I think they may become mortal allies."

"When will he return?"

"Lionel, I'm sending you to go bring him back. I can't spare the both of you, so Hugh, you'll stay here."

"Very good, sir. How will I find him? You have the location?"

"They will be sending you a signal to guide you. It's a frequency only your species can hear."

"We've had it! I woke up to it this morning," gasped Hugh.

"Good. I will let Paolo know, then. You can leave whenever you are ready, Lionel. But don't linger there. Use your mental gifts to alert Hugh to anything dangerous. And be careful. It could be a trap."

Lionel considered his options before he committed to the mission. His mind wandered to the bedroom of a certain mortal woman again. Hugh felt it, staring back in horror at him, and shook his head.

His duty and honor to the Monteleone family was his primary directive, and at last he sighed, resolute with his decision. "I'll leave within the hour. I'll make sure Hugh is fully made aware of my progress." He hesitated and then added. "Marcus, promise me you'll add extra detail to your family and that of the young Dominichelli woman. I have reason to feel you are all in danger, and if I am gone, it will seem like an opportunity to some."

Hugh frowned now, his hands on his hips, his legendary cock swinging almost to his knees.

"I'll take your advice and act on it, Lionel. Thank you for the protection of my family. Please keep yourself out of danger. If it wasn't Jeb, I'd not send you. But I couldn't let you sacrifice your brother. I couldn't ask that of you."

"I understand. I will return intact and with Jeb, in whatever form he remains."

After the call was ended, Hugh punched him in the stomach, sending him rolling backwards, upturning a lamp and small chair. His anger roared, and his fists sought to smash his own flesh and blood, but he stopped short.

"What are you thinking? What were those visions?" Hugh demanded.

"I'm dealing with it." Lionel turned to begin gathering things for his trip. He was looking for the healing bag they carried with them everywhere. Hugh blocked the doorway.

"Was that what I felt it was?"

Lionel looked up to him, feeling guilty and unable to mask his shame.

"I am unable to control it, brother. It's like a—"

Hugh was on him, covering his mouth. "Do not speak of it, brother! It's blasphemy to say it."

"I'm going to find a way to set it aside. Perhaps not eliminate it, but set it aside, to the back of my mind, where it can't hurt me, or—" He stopped, unable to speak her name for fear the dragon of lust building inside him would get loose and wreak havoc with his soul and the souls of both his brothers.

Hugh stepped away and watched him glumly gather things. He only needed a small backpack, enough to bring a cloaking cape in an emergency, some implements like silver handcuffs he had to gingerly handle with heavy work gloves he stuck in there as well. He used a dirty shirt to pick up a string of small silver chain, along with the herbal salve and the healing bag. He fingered over the lavender drawstring pouch with the distinctive letter M embroidered on the top, done by the nimble and impossibly tiny pink fingers of Maria Monteleone herself.

"It is not her, brother," Hugh said, watching Lionel's preoccupation with the stitching.

"You are right. It is not her." He knew Maria Monteleone was dust and bones over two hundred years ago. "But the girl is of her bloodline, I can tell. And you know what we say in Marcus' house."

"Yes. *Blood never lies*," Hugh whispered. "But, what is the *truth*?"

Lionel reached, gripping his brother's shoulder. "Two days ago, I could have told you. Two days ago, I didn't see these things or feel the burning in my gut. Two days ago, Jeb was dead and buried. We were attending that wedding, and the world was dangerous, but manageable." He paused, squeezing the muscles on his brother's upper arm, feeling the strength and power of this magnificent creature he was lucky to call brother. "But today my truth is a journey, a dangerous one, and something I hope I survive. Whether I go or stay behind, it is just as dangerous, Hugh. I can only tackle one mystery at a time. If I survive the first, I'll come back to attend to the other one. In the meantime, keep the ones we love safe from harm."

Hugh embraced him timidly, due to his state of undress. "Consider it done."

Chapter 6

PHOEBE FELT ILL as the first light of morning broke into her room. Her legs became heavy, like made of concrete, causing her to stumble out of bed and barely make it to the bathroom. Her attendant found her with her head in the toilet bowl.

"Oh, little one. I should get your mother. Are you ill?"

"I'm just sick. I have the flu or something."

The room was spinning in all directions. The taste of her vomit was especially bitter, reflecting the deep brownish red contents lying in the bottom of the toilet bowl.

Her mother rushed to her side with a warm towel.

"Phoebe, oh honey. Let's get you up and back to bed."

She brushed her face with the warm towel, but Phoebe's thirst drove her to the sink where she cupped her hands and drank water from the tap. She noticed her throat was raw and sore.

"You are warm again. Do you have a fever?"

She felt her forehead and confirmed what her mother deduced. "I have a sore throat too, and yes, I think I have a fever." She examined herself in the mirror. Her eyes were rimmed in red, her nose was running. The acrid taste was still lingering in her mouth, so she brushed her teeth and began to feel better.

Her mother was fussing to pin her hair up and she stopped her.

"Quit. Just leave it. I need to rest."

"Yes, I think that's best. I'm going to call for the doctor. Here, let's get you back and covered, but first a fresh nightgown." she said, helping Phoebe remove the wet gown and replacing it with a freshly laundered one. She climbed back into her soaking sheets.

Under the circumstances, the coolness of the damp sheets was welcome, and while she listened to her mother and the attendant make plans to remake the bed, she drifted off.

IT WAS LATER in the day when she awoke at last. She could hear voices coming from downstairs, and then the door opened to her room. Dr. Luciano entered, his hat in hand, clutching his black physician's bag. He'd always reminded her of a little mouse, with his small spectacles, grey frizzy hair, and long sideburns. Like a character from a Dicken's novel.

"Bella, Phoebe. Your mother tells me you are unwell," he said as he approached the bed. "May I?" he gestured toward the edge.

"Please."

He sat, repositioning his glasses and taking her pulse. He examined her eyes, frowning, which made his glasses slip so he had to reset them across the bridge of his nose. "Is there any pain here?" he asked as he took her wrist and pressed the veins there.

"No."

"Here?" he asked as he pressed the side of her neck under her ear.

She shrank away from his touch, uneasy to let him see the old bite mark there. "No," she whined and moved away. "It's my stomach."

He turned to ask for help from Freya. He carefully lifted her nightgown to just below her breasts, adjusting the covers down so he could examine her midriff above her navel. He pressed two cold fingers down into her stomach cavity and she felt a sharp pain, followed by a gagging reflex. He listened with a stethoscope to the right of her belly button and then through her nightgown at her upper chest. He pressed his fingers again on the right, and again, she felt pain.

"So you are tender there? What kind of a pain is it? Sharp? Or dull?"

"Sort of in-between. Like I have gas. I feel bloated."

"Ah, yes."

"Dr. Luciano, you should examine the wound. It's nearly healed, but perhaps this is related to some resulting infection?" Freya asked.

"May I, please?"

Phoebe turned her face and pulled down the eyelet lace around her neck to expose the old wound. She felt his cold fingers manipulating the puckered pink flesh of her neck beneath her left ear. He felt for a pulse and nodded.

"I'd like to see the cream you've been using," he asked.

Freya returned from the bathroom and showed him the green vial of salve. He sniffed it and felt it between his two fingers and his thumb, sniffing it again.

"Is there something wrong, doctor?"

"No. Everything seems normal. The healing is re-markable, and there's no issue of infection at the wound site, but something has gotten into her blood-stream and is making her sick. She was given an infusion?"

"Yes, her father's blood."

"Well, that would explain the quick healing. Did she receive more than one feeding?"

"Doctor, she is unturned, so we gave her only one."

"I realize, Freya." He replaced her nightie and drew the covers up to her chin. "I think there is a chance that it was too much for her system. Perhaps she's more delicate than we often see."

Phoebe was concerned. "I've been having strange dreams, too, and my—" She felt her breasts and discovered the swelling had reduced and beneath the cotton fabric of her nightgown her skin didn't feel as tender. "I had other skin irritations, but they seem to be gone now."

"Well, my dear, you're a strong young lady, but not quite strong enough for your father's pure bloodline, at least at this time. I think you overdosed a bit on your family's love." He stood, chuckling, and then addressed Freya. "I wish I could say the same of some others of your clan. Things are so watered down these days."

"You wish to see the contents of what she threw up?" Freya asked him.

When he returned from the bathroom, he smiled. "I think my diagnosis earlier is spot on. You did the right thing by giving her a feeding, but I'd limit this if the need should arise again. I think she took on too much."

Freya was distracted with some distant thought.

"I think you'll be better tomorrow. I'd stay in bed and drink lots of liquids. You're thirsty?"

"Yes, very."

"All normal. Drink broth or something very bland. Herbal tea, if you like. Jell-O?" He grinned. "All the things you liked as a child, my dear."

Phoebe smiled back at him. He'd remembered her favorite was lime Jell-O.

He handed the salve back to Freya. "And let's hold off on this for a day or two until she feels more herself. It's closed the wound and fought infection. Now we let the body do its natural thing."

Her mother tucked the salve into her skirt pocket and nodded her agreement.

He turned to go, giving Phoebe a wink.

"Thank you, doctor."

"Rest, my dear. Rest is your friend. Forget the strange dreams and just rest. That's what you need."

AROUND DUSK, PHOEBE awoke again. The fire had been stoked while she was sleeping and now felt oppressively warm. She pulled back the sheets to air them out and found a small spot of fresh blood on the bottom sheet no larger than the size of a silver dollar. She was frozen in place. As was common with Goldens, she hadn't begun to menstruate since that was a symptom of fating and not usually a natural event for young Golden girls.

She tore the sheets from her bed and scrubbed the remnants of the bloody stain on her feather mattress. But she couldn't remove it entirely, so she flipped the mattress over, pulled fresh sheets from her closet, and remade the bed quickly. She scrubbed the dirty sheet with her hairbrush and got most of it out with soap and cold water, leaving them in a pile in the corner of her bedroom.

She added her soaked nightgown to the pile and stepped into the shower. The warm water soothed her nerves and took the chill from her soul. She scrubbed everywhere, including between her legs, relieved to find no further evidence of bleeding.

She put on her favorite pair of sloppy jeans and an oversized sweatshirt. She pulled her wet hair up on top of her head in a clip, applied some lip gloss and moisturizer, and decided to head downstairs to spend time with the rest of the family. Her brother was due to come home soon, possibly today, and she didn't want to sleep through the homecoming.

At the bathroom doorway, she nearly tripped on the flowered shawl that had comforted her and even protected her two days prior. She drew it to her nose and sniffed, detecting the pungent musky smell of the dark vamp who had saved her life. The hair at the back of her neck stood to attention as the familiar scent continued to bring her comfort.

But she decided to take another action. She threw the shawl on top of the pile of dirty sheets and exited the room, closing the door on that chapter from the wedding.

She was feeling like her old self. It was time to move on with the rest of her life.

Chapter 7

L IONEL TRACED ALONG the whistle sound, bouncing off the edges of the sonar vibration. He found if he stayed just slightly outside the strongest signal he was more conscious of his surroundings. At times, it was difficult to hold back his desire to make the trip at full tracing speed, but managed to slow down, since he wasn't sure what he'd find when he showed up. If it weren't for the fact that his brother's health was at stake, he'd have taken the even more prudent route to go on foot and be preceded by an advanced guard. He wished he'd been able to bring some of the former SEALs his brother had trained.

He'd judged correctly that the night would be in full bloom once he arrived in the desert, where he traced between campsites, clumps of trees, and ancient ruins for cover. He was careful to watch the moon's arc, so he would have time to find a dark space for his sleep requirements. He could push the envelope and go without sleep for one day, provided he didn't use the extra energy to fend off light. But two days could leave him too weakened to make the return trip home.

He scouted caves in stony outcroppings along his journey. But judging from the quality of the beacon tone, he would be traveling across smooth sand, with nothing but man-made temporary shelters to protect him. That was an unacceptable risk under most circumstances. It required he calculate the distance and time factor to Jeb's location first and then await a full dusk to dawn timeframe for his extraction and trip home.

At last, he came upon a cluster of brightly-colored tents lit by campfires. Herds of camel moved restlessly between a watering hole and the vicinity of their keepers. Though it was midnight, Lionel observed the crowd of strangers who moved slowly across sandy peaks and valleys, ducking under layers of heavy carpet. It was obvious they were getting ready to move while the night was still upon them.

He sent out a mental signal to Jeb and didn't get a response. He was going to wait until the next moon when something wafted past him and caught his keen sense of smell. The hair on his arms began to stiffen, his preternatural warning sign. Again, he called to his brother with a low frequency, mental message, and this time heard a faint squeak that was familiar. The signal duplicated the length of his, but the sound was undefined in terms of words.

He drew closer to the source, which led him to a large red tent surrounded by bright orange and yellow flags and long purple streamers. A dozen dark horses nervously whinnied and pulled against their tethers nearby.

He cloaked himself and traced through the fabric, finding an outer tent housing several smaller animals tied to stakes driven in the ground. Wind moaned through the tunnels of the large tent and made his bones chill. He smelled blood—a mixture of vampire as well as mortal blood. He also smelled death.

Lionel was at a crossroads. He was concerned that the element of surprise was not on his side, so it felt dangerous to remain. But he knew Jeb was close by. The air was pregnant with a pattern he heard between the whistling of the winds over the sand as it splashed up against the walls. He risked sending a message to Hugh, with a warning he feared he'd fallen into a trap.

He listened, tuning carefully to the vibration while keeping his cloaking device from scaring the small animals. At last, he heard the plea for help from Jeb, coming like air through a small reed. It was mostly the sound of breathing but laced between were definitely vocal sounds. And then he felt the mind pattern, and his heart warmed to the knowledge that Jeb was indeed alive. But very weak and broken.

"Come in, traveler," came the clipped voice of a stranger behind him. Lionel was sure the cloaking was still functioning, so he turned to find a giant of a dark man smiling down on him. His robed arm lifted a carpeted curtain, revealing a golden glow and warmth inside.

Lionel remained frozen in place. He tapped down his apprehension and tried not to react to the invitation given him. He could not afford to trust the man, even with Jeb nearby. Until he could make communication with him, he wasn't going to move.

The giant began to laugh. "You think I talk to myself?"

Lionel traced to a space behind the dark shadow, who didn't turn in response, seemingly unable to adjust to his movement.

He sent out another message to Jeb and recognized the answering silent scream.

"*Run!*"

Lionel immediately traced to the opposite side of the tent and stopped, controlling his breathing, his thoughts and even the speed at which his preternatural blood was flowing. He pressed out any of the images of his journey, images of his recent past. Instead, he concentrated on scenes from his childhood, visions of him and his brothers playing as mortal children before their turning.

He heard his brother sob as the visions reached him. That gave Lionel the coordinates he needed. He traced and found Jeb lying in a heap of bloody rags. Just as Marcus had told, Jeb had been draped in bandages, which were seeping with some mixture that included blood. The smell was foul.

Jeb was missing one lower arm, which was wrapped as far as his elbow joint, which appeared in working order. But his arms were thin, and several places revealed raw bone the bandages failed to cover. Both his legs were there, but cast at odd angles, and obviously not useable in their present state. Like leaves scattered in the fall, pieces of blackened flaky skin littered the ground all around him.

Lionel knew it was Jeb, because he felt his lifeforce, but the skull that angled up toward him was unrecognizable. He was missing eyes, the dark caverns hollowly staring up at him as if he could still see.

"No," Jeb began to whisper. "Go away. Save yourself." His lips could barely form words, and his speech was more slurred than spoken. But the danger in those words was impossible to miss.

Suddenly, a large silver cage dropped from the ceiling and trapped both brothers inside. While hearing the sound of evil laughter echoing throughout his cell, Lionel took stock of the room by dim torchlight and noted the source of the awful smell. Rotting corpses lay strewn about, most of them shriveled and burned to a crisp. Various metal implements and spears with silver tips eerily reflected the dancing flames.

Knowing the silver would prevent him from any type of action, Lionel stared down at the frame of his brother shivering at his feet. The trap had been sprung, and now the rescuer was the prey in need of saving. He could not help but feel his heart breaking at what could become of them both.

HE CALMLY ASSESSED his status. If he was lured to Jeb's side to be executed, it would have happened by now. No, Lionel thought, he was being caught alive, not because of *who* he was but *what* he was.

He held Jeb's face up off the bloody rags, sliced one of his own wrists open with his teeth, and dropped some of his blood inside his brother's gaping mouth, rubbing it over Jeb's gums and lips. Instantly, Jeb's skin began to change color and then shape. Under the golden light of the torch, he watched as portions of Jeb's bones were covered in muscle, veins, arteries, and then pink flesh protecting the network of nutrient delivery. His arm healed, restoring some of his muscle tissue, all the way to the elbow, and then ended in a puckering stump that broke free of the bandages.

Lionel knew time was not on his side, but he was hoping that just enough of it would help bring Jeb to a form able to help in his own escape, if the opportunity arrived.

Jeb's thoughts were streaming past him. Lionel saw visions of the bonfire of Jeb's entwined body, clutching Dag's crispy form, even grappling with the mere skeleton of Dag as it tried to slither across the sand in the hot noon sun. He saw Jeb awaken, felt the terror and the pain that he was on fire. Later, he saw Jeb being tended to, huddled at the bottom of an ornate cage as if made for a large pet bird or monkey.

Or a pet vampire.

He sent out a healing message as the blood from his wrist dribbled down over his brother's lips and onto his chest.

I've seen it, Jeb. Now drink. Be whole. I am here, Brother.

Eyelids formed, covering the vacant caverns where his tender brown eyes had once been. And when they opened, he saw that Jeb's sight had been restored. The twisted smile from thin lips that barely covered his teeth and gums was one of the most beautiful things Lionel had ever seen.

The heavy laughter coming from overhead turned his veins ice cold. Jeb coughed up and attempted to right himself to sitting position, using his arm stump. Lionel left his wrist against his brother's mouth but looked up at the evil face of his captor.

"Welcome, Lionel Jett. I am so happy to see you earning your keep. It's been expensive keeping your brother alive. He has a strong will to live."

"As do I," Lionel challenged him.

"I can see that."

"State your purpose." Lionel reverted to his warrior frame of mind.

"To make a trade."

"But I have nothing to offer," Lionel barked.

"Oh, but you do," the large man laughed. Gold in his teeth glistened, and a large ring hung from one torn earlobe. A scar slashed across his otherwise smooth and weathered face creating a permanent scowl of his upper lip. His gnarled fingers were adorned with shiny jeweled rings, and his wrists were encrusted in dozens of gold bands, which jingled as he pointed to Lionel's wrist at Jeb's mouth.

Lionel knew this man was mortal, but under the weight of the silver bars, even the strength of both he and his brother combined, if they were both healthy, would be no match for the mortal enemy. It would mean a waiting game of opportunity before he was reduced to flakes and charred bones like that which now surrounded him.

He was hoping, even incanting a small prayer, to be underestimated. He wondered how much of the night he had left. He wondered if any of his mental messages to Hugh had gotten through. With the silver in place, this would no longer be possible.

"So name your terms, captor."

"You act like you have some say in the matter." He chuckled while pulling up a stool and stared down at the two of them. "I am Salaman, and I control everything in this place you can see with your eyes. I'll show you when it's light. From one horizon, to the other, all mine."

Lionel couldn't help but flinch.

Salaman continued. "Yes, I know you fear the sun. So perhaps that won't be possible, but never mind. As I was saying, I am looking for a trade. And you, Lionel Jett, are part of the bargain, not a party to the negotiations. You are a valuable commodity."

Lionel could only imagine several parties who might be interested in negotiating for their release. Certainly, the Monteleones would pay handsomely, or he hoped they would. If the price wasn't too dear.

"I have spoken to your employer. He is aware you have arrived. He is also aware of the condition of your brother."

Jeb began to sit upright, pushing away Lionel's wrist. His ears were growing back before Lionel's eyes, his breathing deepened, but his legs were still emaciated and not able to hold his weight. His mind, though, was returning. Lionel could see Jeb was interested in the conversation now, just as much as he was.

Salaman smiled, revealing his golden canines. His gaze was hungry, as if what he was about to say was so delicious he nearly drooled. He leaned forward, placing his weight on his oversized forearms piled atop his tree stump knees covered in heavy robes.

"What I want is what has been stolen from me. I have studied your kind for a very long time. I have imprisoned hundreds, enjoyed, well—" He waved over the detritus that rotted around them all. "I have a taste for your kind. But I crave the Golden bloodlines even more. I've had difficulty obtaining them."

He leaned back on his stool and crossed his arms with a smug tight-lipped smile.

"He will not give you what you want," Lionel spat back.

"Oh, I think he will."

"You know he would never sacrifice a Golden for one of us, and I would never stand for it, either."

"You're the bait. The bargain. You have no say."

"No, I'm a living being who will fight you till the death. And then what will you have?"

"So I find another. Eventually, I will find a nice, ripe Golden. Perhaps a virgin? Would he not sacrifice one to save the family? You are an important part of his protection, even his family."

Lionel was struck with the realization that some of the confidential information they'd discussed in the Monteleone library was now privy to Salaman. There was a betrayal within the family, and Marcus was unaware of this.

He could feel Jeb's thoughts. He was searching the perimeter of the cage, inspecting for some weak spot. Some way out.

Quiet, brother.

But I'm nearly thin enough to get through these bars.

No.

Their private conversation didn't appear to faze Salaman in any fashion. That told Lionel that they now had a good weapon to use, once Jeb was fully restored. He reached over and righted first one leg and then the other, squeezing to feel evidence of some healing, and did sense a tiny vibration beginning to build.

"I understand your desire for a Golden," Lionel began.

"*Unsullied* Golden."

"As you say," Lionel repeated and extended his wrist to Jeb again. "But surely you have a second request, perhaps a compromise."

Salaman laughed and stood, kicking the stool to the corner. "Right you are, vampire! But what I haven't told you is that a virgin Golden female *is* my second choice." He waited.

Lionel was full of dread.

"I want the book your employer has. I desire to own the book that was destined to become mine. I think you know it. It's called *The Book of Spawn*."

Chapter 8

PHOEBE WAS JOINED by several men from Marcus' protective detail. Her cousin, Paolo, was there to introduce them to her, one by one.

"Your mother has asked me to acquaint you with some young gentlemen we employ. Marcus and I have decided you should be able to choose your protection."

She darted a look to her mother, who remained stoic. Phoebe could tell she'd been crying.

"My protection? Not—?"

"Not yet, Daughter," her father interrupted. He turned his attention to Paolo. "Phoebe and her mother have discussed many options with me for her protection."

She held her breath, hoping her father wouldn't betray much of their personal conversation. She was relieved when he stopped.

Paolo continued. "As you know, we've trained these gentlemen, who were former Special Forces Operators, mostly former SEALs."

Phoebe watched as several of the men inhaled, extending their chests out. They were well-built, clean shaven, and none of them gave off any sort of disrespect to her, even accounting for her lack of experience or age. They stared straight ahead. All but one.

The only man in the lineup who looked at her was the dark vamp she'd seen the day of the wedding, the one who shared the protection of Paolo's son, Lucius. As soon as their eyes met, he averted his gaze away.

Phoebe stared longingly at her mother for direction. "How many do I choose? I don't know how to make the selection. Mother—" She ran to her mother's side, whispering, "I wasn't prepared to do this tonight. How am I supposed to do this?"

"No cause for alarm, Phoebe." Freya nodded to the line of men and, without asking for input from her husband, said, "Please pick three."

Paolo gasped.

Her husband added, "Wait, Freya. I don't think Marcus expected—"

But Paolo whisked her away into the garden room off the kitchen where Phoebe could hear their argument. She examined each of the men, noticing tattoos and scars, the size of their muscled arms, how they nervously swallowed or moved their fingers. Though she was very close as she passed by each of them, none made eye contact. She was fascinated with little variations in their form, the fullness of their lips, the color of their eyes, and their scent. Some wore cologne and others smelled of soap and shave cream. One of them had cut himself doing so. Another had a band aid over his third finger knuckle.

She wondered if any of them danced, what they looked like when they played a game of catch or rode a bicycle. She wondered if her mother would ever let her kiss one of them, or perhaps two.

If I had to choose a husband, which one would it be? How could I ever tell? I don't feel the pulling in my gut or my breath getting heavy. The hairs at the back of my neck and my upper arms don't stand out. My mouth isn't parched nor is it overly wet. My heartbeat isn't rapid, and I am not sweating. None of the things that happened before are happening now.

Why?

As she ended her slow perusal of the line of men, she stood before the large dark vamp who was with her that day at the wedding. Noticing she also didn't have a physical reaction to his presence, she asked him,

"And you are Hugh Jett."

"Yes, Miss," he returned softly. He did not meet her gaze.

"But your brother calls you something else."

"Yes, Miss. He often calls me Brother."

"Not that," she said carefully. "He has another first name he calls you. I've heard it."

Some of the men began to snicker and one coughed into his fist.

"Yes, Miss. He sometimes calls me—Huge."

Now three men stepped out of line and coughed, each taking a second to compose themselves before returning to the column. Hugh's eyelids were halfway closed, and Phoebe could see he didn't like being toyed with and was masking being annoyed.

Her father stepped beside her. "Phoebe, this is no game. We are serious about your welfare."

Just as her mother and Paolo returned, Phoebe reached for the hand of the former military man who had the tattoo of a mermaid on his forearm. "I chose you." Then she walked to Hugh and also took his hand. "And I pick Huge."

She turned and surveyed the shocked expression on her mother's face.

"Only two. This mortal for daytime, and one for night."

ARRANGEMENTS WERE MADE for the two of them to report to the villa tomorrow evening, where Samuel would be given a room on the second floor across from Phoebe's, since Hugh had quarters he shared with his brother off site. It would also serve as their base of operation.

They'd be given a tour of the grounds and all the rooms, even the private rooms of the Dominichelli family only servants were allowed in. Preparations were made to go over house security, the necessary vetting of all the household staff, some of their intimate family rules and customs and their upcoming travel plans, including when Phoebe's two brothers would return home.

Before they could complete the instructions, Paolo received a call from his brother and had to return home with his men.

Phoebe didn't miss the whisper her cousin gave to Hugh, which set his face ashen. As he tore from the room, he neglected to say good-bye.

She walked behind her parents as they entered the warm kitchen area. Their cook gave Phoebe another bowl of chicken broth, and she was grateful for her kindness.

"You are better?" her mother asked, sifting her fingers through Phoebe's long hair and attempting to re-tie her ribbon.

She nodded. "No more stomachache. I felt well

enough to change my own sheets."

"Wonderful." Freya said as she hugged her. Feeling her forehead, she remarked, "And your fever is down. I think Dr. Luciano was correct in his diagnosis."

Phoebe's father rolled his eyes and then his shoulders.

"What was all that with Marcus? Did you hear?" Freya asked him.

"I wasn't given that information. A family matter. I think it had to do with Hugh's brother."

"That's Lionel. His name is Lionel," whispered Phoebe.

The sound of his name spoken left a pleasant taste in her mouth.

SHE STAYED UP with her mother, working together on hand top-stitching a quilt that was to be presented to another marrying couple. A wedding band quilt, the pattern was that of many concentric and interloping circles. Phoebe preferred square, more balanced patterns of color, but the design was a tradition in her family and would be displayed proudly for generations to come.

"So, just to be clear, I am not picking a husband."

"Correct. Although you could always change your mind."

"I feel nothing for any of them. I don't even know them."

"Friendships between male and female are difficult and sometimes strange. They take years to develop properly sometimes. Best to become friends now, then companions later."

"So you had friends? You know they now call them friends with benefits?" Phoebe felt wicked for making her mother throw down her needlework.

"Honestly, Phoebe. There is a streak in you I'm not pleased to see develop."

"But you've told me I have to remain strong, to learn to defend myself. I don't want to leave my future in someone else's hands, even if it is yours and Father's. Maybe I'm just beginning to experiment with taking over the reins I'll have to wield."

"I accept your apology," Freya retorted with a huff.

Phoebe sighed and squinted to see the edges of fabric she was supposed to follow. Within seconds, her eyes filled with tears.

Though the effects of the attack and her father's infusion were gone, the lingering apprehension remained in her chest that the world had tilted three days ago, and her life would forever be altered. New things would be expected of her—things she'd never encountered. And her family support network was also changing. She began to feel it drifting away. Her place safely embedded between her parents, their only daughter and the special one of the family, was somehow being dislodged.

It was a bit like playing hide-and-seek with the blindfold on. Except this wasn't a child's game any longer. There were life and death consequences to winning or losing.

Over the silence that spread past several minutes, she wondered how it would feel to have a male protector outside her bedroom door. It had always been her father, and now it was going to gradually become some stranger. And both these new protectors were of different species, with backgrounds different than her own. Would they understand her? Or, could she learn from them?

She told her mother she was tired and retreated upstairs. Before entering her bedroom, she opened the small guest room that would be soon occupied. In the daytime, it had a glorious view of her mother's gardens and the rolling vineyards beyond. A writing desk stood in front of the window, with one of the hand-made journals her father liked to make and an antique fountain pen with the Dominichelli crest on the side in gold. She fingered the book, loving the smooth texture of the imported paper her father used.

To her right was the enormous four-poster bed that she'd always coveted, but her mother saved for only special guests.

"It's not a proper bed for a young lady, Phoebe," her mother had said.

The opulent designs over the headboard and the vines carved in relief along the four heavy columns that held the burgundy tapestry canopy had always been a curiosity to her. Even as a small child, she'd loved to trace the figurines and make up stories of what could have been or what might have happened centuries ago.

Some nights, she snuck into the room and slept there, returning to her own chamber before daylight. She dreamt she was the queen of a kingdom that adored her.

Phoebe tore herself away from her childhood fantasies and returned to her room, to the warmth of the well-provisioned fire, the glowing bright white sheets lovingly laid back for her, and the pillows plumped and ready for her head.

The dirty pile of sheets in the corner was gone, but the shawl was laid across an iron grate and was drying by the fireplace, having been washed by hand.

As she scanned the room, she noticed the window had been barred shut, and knew this was intentional. Gone would be her nights staring at the stars or dreaming in the moonlight. These were dangerous days ahead. She'd need a good dose of courage, as well as logic, to figure out the maze that was coming upon her. It was a race that didn't leave her much time to win. Perhaps not nearly enough time.

She slipped into the covers and fell back on the pillows, waiting. She wanted to remember the tranquility of this night, the way it felt to know what she knew, just before she began her next adventure. It was the calm before the storm.

Just as she drifted off to sleep, she touched her lips and felt the word spoken into the warm night air as she uttered it.

"Lionel."

Chapter 9

"EVEN IF HE had it, and he's claimed he doesn't, Marcus would never trade that book for us, brother." Lionel had paced for an hour after Salaman left. During that time, Jeb had inspected each rung of the silver bars, top to bottom, still looking for a weakness.

"You're going to worry yourself to death, Lionel. Stop with the pacing. Rest. Save your strength for some useful mental exercise."

"I should have foreseen this, Jeb. I blame myself. And now we have almost no time left. It must be close to dawn. I've failed Marcus, Paolo—all of them."

"Marcus has resources, brother. And he has friends. Look at me." He spread his arms to the side, displaying his stub on one side and his outstretched hand on the other. With difficulty, he stood without using the silver bars for balance, which would have caused another burn he didn't need. He hopped, favoring his left leg, until he could put half his weight on it. "See?"

"You are far from being able to save us, Jeb. You need more time to heal."

"But look at me, Brother. I had given up all hope. I never thought I'd see your face again. Yet here we are. Not like it used to be, but much has changed since you arrived. I can risk feeling hopeful again. You've brought that to me." He lowered his head and wiggled his eyebrows. "I might even hope to find some sardines!"

"God in Heaven, Jeb. We're in the middle of the desert. The Sahara Desert."

"Hope springs eternal. What I'm saying, Brother, is that you've given me hope for a future I'd completely given up on."

"Yes, by placing myself on the altar as a sacrificial lamb."

"No, not sacrificial. You are the object of desire, brother. You were meant to be desired. If it is your last thought, remember that."

Lionel didn't like the direction of the conversation. "I desire to escape, brother. That is all I desire."

"Not that kind of desire, Lionel. I've seen her."

Lionel shot his brother a dangerous look.

"You've met the new Maria. The one you never thought you could have," Jeb whispered, trying to smile. His lips still looked shriveled and taught.

Lionel saw the angelic face of young Maria Monteleone, unchanged by years of mortal decay. He could almost taste her.

"*That* one, Brother. The one you denied yourself once. Who is she?"

"I won't speak of it."

"*Tell* me. If I can feel it in my weakened condition, something is important there."

Finally, Lionel resigned himself to divulge his secret. "She's a Dominichelli, but Maria's a many times great grandmother, so she has Monteleone blood in her veins on her mother's side. I think it's her appearance that has me so haunted."

"Haunted? No, Brother. It isn't a haunting you feel."

"Stop it, Jeb. I've put it out of my mind."

"Like Hell you have. I can feel her all over your insides, Lionel. You carry her scent. Any preternatural being could feel it as well."

Lionel hadn't thought he was thinking that transparently.

"Are you going to allow this evil salesman to steal your right to a life of devoted love?"

"It's blasphemy. We won't discuss it any longer."

"No. Make it the *reason* to survive, Lionel. You'd die to protect Marcus, and Paolo and the wives and children—Lucius and his progeny to come. But her? She is your *reason to live*."

The words hit Lionel in the gut and forced him to sit down hard. He'd been steeling his chest, holding back any emotion, but now the full import of his regret, the years of mourning one woman only to be given a chance with another, became too heavy to bear. He'd only shed tears twice in his life. The first time was when young Maria told him she was going to remain mortal, but that she wanted him as her protector. She had said she did not have any right to ask it of him. He'd cried that night.

The second time was as the seconds of her life slipped away under the stars as he held her frail body before it left on its journey to her Heaven. If she'd but asked him, he'd have given her immortality, but that wasn't her wish. She chose to spend eternity with her husband who had gone before her. Lionel remembered the shock and pain of understanding he had not been chosen.

The hot tears that coursed down his cheeks were heavy, but they fell silently like snow.

Jeb's face appeared in front of him, waking him from his morose dreams. "I said live, Lionel. Think—

no, *feel*—the will to live. To find her and to protect her."

As Lionel studied his brother's eyes, he understood that love was stronger than duty or honor. Or sacrifice. He no longer felt it was a betrayal he'd feel guilty over.

As if they'd together conjured it from thin air, several young women covered from head to toe in traditional nomadic garb appeared. Between them there were whispers of an unfamiliar language using a series of tongue clicks. A brown bony hand extended through the bars, dropping several large pieces of cloth at their feet. Jeb sniffed the fabric, wrapping it around his arm, then covering his head. He began swathing his body with more fabric given by other hands.

"Do it, brother," Jeb whispered. "Cover yourself."

One of the women demonstrated the wrapping, extending her arms through the silver to adjust and secure fabric covering their faces everywhere except for their eyes. They were encouraged to stand. Lionel held Jeb's waist, looking above his head and hearing a metal clanging sound as the cage was lifted several feet, enough so that he could bend and get free, pulling Jeb behind him across the floor.

The women whispered and motioned for them to follow.

An opening was made to the outside. Lionel could

see the pink dawn fast approaching, and he shook his head. Jeb's body had already tensed up, his new skin becoming sensitive to the light penetrating the fabric. Lionel also felt burning begin at the edges of his eyes where there was no protection.

A cloth was placed over his head, but the pain seemed to come from his insides out as his flesh simmered, sending smoke to his nostrils and making him cough dizzyingly. He felt the press of a woman's body against his and then another, clawing and clutching at him, constricting his movements.

"Jeb," he whispered, unable to see.

"You must trace us home. I will help all I can. I'm—" Jeb's voice ended in a deep muffled moan sounding like he was biting his own arm to keep from screaming.

Lionel again felt the press of bodies and then the firm hand of his brother. He mentally reached low into his own chest and felt his heart muscle expand to near bursting, matching his conscious intention and an inner resolve he'd never felt before. The strength and power of his ancient species filled him.

He bit his lip, tasting blood, and held his breath as young Phoebe's face came to him. He knew he'd be losing consciousness within seconds but concentrated on getting as close to her as possible. If he could build momentum, this force might complete his journey home while unconscious.

In a ball of fire, while encumbered by all the attachments of those who clung to him, he hurled through the sky like a comet.

His strength gave out mere seconds later as he fell into a pool of water, which turned to steam all around him. The weight of the fabric pulled him down as he desperately struggled for air. He began shedding the arms and legs that had hold of him, removing everything that was an impediment. Beneath the water, he could hear his brother scream. He rolled over, dragging Jeb with him until he felt land beneath his feet.

The pink sky was now turning brighter and becoming blue as his skin continued to combust where it came in contact with the light. Olive branches overhead still smoldered with fire. Jeb was dead weight to him. In his weakened condition he could not drag his brother out of the bright light and into shade. He felt skin slough off and burn his palms as he tried.

Dark splotches formed in front of his eyes just before he felt arms pull him under the shoulders and then lift him into a dark box smelling of diesel. He suddenly realized he was in a lorry or van of some kind. The gracious metal clanging doors at last put him into complete darkness.

He hung onto his consciousness long enough to hear someone make the comment, "It's Jeb. He's brought Jeb back from the dead."

LIONEL WOKE TO the awful acrid smell of burning flesh. His flesh. He opened his eyes and could not see a thing. His fingers explored his face and confirmed he'd not lost his eyes. His skin was slippery, covered in salve, which stung and made him tear up.

Carefully, he inhaled as deeply as he could, then let the air out slowly. Judging how much control he had with his own breathing, he was satisfied he was going to survive.

His preternatural sight was coming back, and he discovered he was in his own room, on the Monteleone estate in Tuscany. He could not remember exactly how he'd gotten there, but he was grateful for the first aid he'd received by loving hands.

He swung his legs off the platform bed and felt the cool wooden floor on his bare feet. One arm and shoulder were wrapped in a tight bandage steeped in something that smelled as terrible as the burning flesh. As he stood, his balance returned, and his thigh muscles began to work holding up his solid frame. However long he'd spent in the early morning light had apparently not burned him all the way to the bone.

But he still hurt all over.

Hearing coughing in the next room, he pushed aside his bedroom door and entered their tiny living room. Jeb's room was occupied at last. He saw light from under the door and burst through.

Paolo and Marcus were shaken at the sudden action and stood at once. By the light of the single candle flame he could see his brother's frail frame. The bones of his chest rose and fell as Jeb was taking air on his own. His face was a bloody mess of bandages and peeling skin. All the hair had been burned off his head.

Lionel began to sway as the room spun out of control. Darkness overtook him as he felt himself fall to the floor.

Because the back of his head hurt, he knew he was not yet dead.

Chapter 10

THE ENTIRE VILLAGE was abuzz with news that Lionel had returned and brought Jeb with him. Like Lazarus being raised from the dead, the next several days were filled with stories of Lionel's heroics.

Phoebe sat with Hugh in the kitchen while she ate her late supper. He'd been talking non-stop. He was so proud of his brother. It was as if the family had needed some good news and clung to every detail.

"So when will he be fully recovered?" she asked.

"He's recovered now! He's tending to Jeb, but my brothers are starting to argue, which is always a good sign."

Phoebe wondered why, if he was well, Lionel didn't come by the house or check in with Hugh at the little room prepared for her protectors. She hoped she wasn't mistaken. She was sure he'd want to see her.

"Maybe I'll bring him some flowers," she whispered, drifting off into a dreamlike state.

Hugh scrunched up his face like a prune. "Lionel?

Flowers?"

"For good health. For speedy recovery."

"If you want that, bring him salve."

"Chicken soup?"

"Phoebe, what's gotten into you? There is nothing you can do. He'll be going back to California with Marcus and Paolo soon, anyway. I'm sure they'll have him busy getting ready for the trip."

She decided she'd waited too long. "Take me there, tonight."

"I'm not allowed. Your parents would never permit that."

"I want to thank him. I never got to properly thank him for my rescue."

"No." Hugh was hugging himself as if cold. "That's a very bad idea. Besides, he was protecting Lucius. Disposing of wayward dark coven vamps, well, we do that all the time. Happening more and more these days."

"Hugh, trace me there."

"That's also forbidden. You heard the doctor's orders. You're not even allowed outside."

"But I'm completely well. I'm eating solid food. I feel—" She suddenly realized her cheeks were flushed and her nipples were once again tender. "I won't be outside. You'll trace me from inside this kitchen to inside your home."

"Not our home."

"The home you were given for your stay."

Hugh cracked his neck and looked upstairs. "Your parents are asleep?"

"They've retired, but I have no idea. We won't be long. Just a quick trip there, and a quick trip back again before anyone misses us."

Hugh was still wrestling with his conscience. Phoebe grabbed his upper arms and pleaded. "Please. A favor for me. One little favor." She held up her thumb and forefinger to demonstrate just how little the favor was. Her smile was warming Hugh's expression.

"I'm going to regret this. I know it for certain."

"Take me," Phoebe sighed, closing her eyes and holding out her arms. She heard Hugh's laughter and spared a glance through her squint.

"Not that way. Here, put your arms around me like we were dancing."

"Which reminds me. Samuel and I are taking dancing lessons. I want you to come as well."

"No. Absolutely not. That's out of the question. As a matter of fact—"

"Okay, okay, no dancing lessons. Let's go."

She wrapped her arms around Hugh's waist and closed her eyes, leaning her head against his chest just beneath his jawline.

The sensation was not unlike being in an elevator. When she opened her eyes, the room was so dark she stumbled into Hugh, who had taken her hand and was leading her into Jeb's bedroom.

Lionel was seated on the bed, placing bandages against Jeb's naked body. His fingers were covered in the greenish salve that had worked so well on her wound. He turned to face her, and she saw him tense, slamming his mouth shut.

"Get her out of here," Lionel shouted. "Right now."

"I know, I know. But the woman is damned convincing. Sorry, I'll just—"

"I came to say thank you to my protector. To the one who helped save my life."

Everyone was stunned until Jeb swore and threw a blanket over his hard-on. "Dammit. I don't want anyone seeing me until I stop looking like a freak!"

Phoebe dropped Hugh's hand and put a palm to her mouth. Tufts of hair were struggling to regrow in patches all over Jeb's scalp. His left arm was missing a forearm and one of his bloody toes was missing.

Something smelled awful, a new sensation for her. She wrinkled up her nose. "Your flesh. When it burns, it smells like fish!"

Jeb began swearing.

Lionel was on her in a flash, closing the door behind him to give his brother privacy. He grabbed her arm and shook her. The pain he'd inflicted was sudden and it scared her. She reflexively slapped him across the face and watched as his eyes flared in anger.

She was angry too. She defiantly yanked herself free from his grip. "You're hurting me. Stop it and let me talk to you."

Lionel turned his back to her. Hugh shrugged, unable to find words.

Phoebe found the courage to step closer to the hulking dark protector and placed her hand on his shoulder blade through the material of his shirt. "Lionel, I mean you no harm. I only wanted to say thank you. I'm happy that your family is reunited." She paused, her hand still rubbing his back. "F-For some reason, I was *called* to see you."

Lionel whipped around, and her hand was left in midair. Until Lionel clasped it in both of his.

"Thank you, dear lady." His eyes were kind, like melted pools of chocolate. She felt the pulse of his heartbeat strong and increasing in speed. She tried to place her palm up to his cheek, but he stopped her.

"It is enough that you come here in person to say thank you."

"Phoebe. Say my name. Phoebe."

He stumbled, at first scanning the ground. "Phoebe," he whispered.

"Lionel," she returned. "Will you come visit with me tomorrow night?"

"I'm not sure that's wise."

"But will you anyway?" She was transfixed by his gentle aura enveloping her like a protective shield. Their fingers had become entwined. As she drank from his eyes, she heard Hugh swear out of the shadows in the corner.

"I-I…"

"Just say yes. Just come for a visit. It's all I'll ask of you tonight. Promise me." She brought his palm to her cheek and drew the answer from him.

"Yes. I'll be there at seven."

HUGH TRACED THEM back to the warm kitchen. "I need a drink."

Phoebe smiled, enjoying the way her skin tingled where Lionel had touched her. She retrieved two goblets from the dining room and poured Hugh a whiskey from her father's rare reserve collection. Then she poured another one for herself.

Hugh downed the liquid and carefully set the crystal glass on the counter. "Not a word. Not to anyone. Not your brothers, your mother or father, not the priest, or to Samuel."

Phoebe was enjoying his squirming. Her heart was filled with joy.

"No worries, Hugh," she said as she touched his cheek.

"Don't." Hugh batted her hand down. "I don't want to be seen anywhere when you touch me, unless I'm lifting you out of a wagon or carriage, or—" He began pacing. "I will rot in Hell for this. I can feel it as sure as I'm standing here."

"Hugh, you only did what I requested. And see, I'm safe. You got me back home safe and sound. No worries. All is forgotten, and no one needs to know."

"But *I'll* know. And Jeb knows what I did as well. I'm going to be discharged from all my duties. I've betrayed the family trust."

"Don't be silly." She ran to the dining room and came back with the whiskey carafe. "More?"

"No. And you shouldn't, either."

"I have to, or I won't sleep."

"Phoebe," Hugh blurted out as he watched her pour another full glass of spirit. "You have to get to bed before anyone in the house discovers you're up. If they ask questions, I won't be able to lie. You know this."

"I do, and I love you for it," she said over her shoulder, feeling the warm glow of the whiskey in her stomach.

"Don't say that. This is no joke."

"Hugh, nothing you can tell me tonight will dampen my mood. I feel positively ancient. I'm the happiest I've ever been." She ran towards him, and he shrank away, pushing his hands out in front for protection.

"Don't *touch* me, Phoebe. I mean it." She could see that Hugh was at a near-panic state.

With her hands on her hips she gave him a stern warning. "I need to talk to him about a couple of things, Hugh. It would have been a tragedy if he left for California without that discussion. That was the urgency. I had to speak to him before he left. That's not so unusual, is it?"

Hugh didn't want to look at her, but he acknowledged her words and even nodded his agreement. "That's the way we'll leave it. Goddammit, you're stubborn!"

His face was lined with worry. She wished she could convince him that all would be well. Now that she'd confirmed some of her deepest secrets, all *would* be well.

It was going to be a bumpy ride, but it wasn't going to take a hundred years, or more, either.

"I'll leave you the bottle while I get to bed. Up to you what happens next. But, from the bottom of my heart, thank you, Hugh." She pressed her palms together as if in prayer, backed out of the room, then danced up the stairs, and shut her door.

Chapter 11

LIONEL HAD TAKEN his shirt off and changed it three times before he removed the tie he had intended to wear and threw it on his bed, leaving his collar open, unbuttoned at the top. He already felt like he had a garrote around his neck.

Jeb leaned against his doorway, stabilizing his frame on a metal crutch.

"Kinda helps you appreciate what Paolo and Marcus went through when they did their ceremony," Jeb whispered.

Lionel turned on him. "There's no fuckin' ceremony. And in about two seconds there will be no meet and greet, either."

Jeb was having trouble keeping a straight face. "What men go through to torture themselves for the women in their lives."

"Stop it, Jeb. Not. Helping."

Lionel asked himself if she was indeed the woman in his life, and the conclusion was a puddle of question marks. The possible fating would have to remain a secret, forever. He thought it prudent to remind his younger brother.

"While I appreciate the pep talk you gave me in North Africa, which also happened to save your backside, I'm not sure I can call her the woman in my life. For me, and you know this,"—He'd pointed to Jeb with two fingers—"there has never been more than one woman in my life. Phoebe is not *her*."

"Go ahead and convince yourself if it makes it easier, Lionel, but I'm not believing a word of it. And for the record, I'll not be speaking about it until it becomes something we can. That I'll give you. But know the truth. You have the fate, which is the joy and the curse of our species, all over you. It's like your head has been reattached to your body, backwards."

Lionel sat on his bed, studying things in his room he'd cherished—things no female had ever seen. Next to his pillow was a miniature painting of the young and healthy Maria Monteleone. It was the first thing he packed when he traveled privately, and the last thing he looked at in the early morning before he turned in for the restorative sleep.

"I am more fearful of today than I was tracing to your location in the Sahara."

"I can see that."

"I harbor a crime deep within my heart. And the repercussions, if it were made public, could also affect you and Hugh."

They shared the private gaze that was so common when one of them or all of them were going off to war or on some dangerous mission. When it was acknowledged that one of them might not survive.

"I don't hold you responsible for things you cannot control. I only hope it happens to me that way."

"It's against everything I've trained for," Lionel stopped him.

"And it's everything a healthy male yearns for. We stand beside you. You'd do it for either of us, Lionel."

He knew his brother was right.

The two brothers embraced and then separated. Lionel kick-started his motorcycle and tore off into the mild, Fall night.

A shopkeeper was doing some nighttime cleanup as he rounded the curve, slowing down to cruise through the back way to the Dominichelli estate. Her colorful roses were still in their stands. He chose yellow ones, hoping they'd be considered safe, allowed the old woman to wrap them in green waxed paper, and stuck them inside his jacket, unzipping the leather just enough to keep the flowers from becoming smashed.

The Dominichelli long, crushed granite driveway

filed through groves of olives, bordered by tall Cypress trees in clumps of three every few meters. In the starlit night, the tall silent beings stood witness to the gauntlet he was about to walk. Like judges or executioners, they showed no emotion as he passed on the most important mission of his lifetime. His last mission, if he'd misjudged.

The heavy carved door with the Dominichelli crest swung inside before he appeared on the stoop. He recognized his brother's bike and a couple of vehicles parked in the yard on the right.

He'd met her mother, Freya, for the first time at the wedding that day. She studied him carefully, blocking the doorway. He knew she couldn't hear his thoughts, so he decided to reassure her to ease the pulsing vein at her temple.

"She has called for me. I hope that you were made aware, Madam Dominichelli," he said as he bowed to her, sending the yellow roses up and into his nostrils.

She held her head at a strange angle and was waiting for him to notice she'd extended her hand for him to kiss. He did so with chaste speed.

He retrieved the roses from his jacket and handed them to the beautiful woman, who smiled at the gesture.

"Lovely. Phoebe will love them. Yellow is one of

her favorite colors." She delicately pushed them back to his chest. "Come, protector. Or, can I call you Lionel?"

"What do you call Hugh?"

She threw her head back as he followed her through the anteroom and into a small hallway leading to the kitchen, which was their traditional gathering place. She smelled wonderful.

"We call him Huge, but I'm not quite sure he's comfortable with it yet. My daughter said she heard you call him that, and somehow, it just stuck."

Lionel cursed under his breath. His voice broke as he spoke. "Then I suppose you could call me Lionel, ma'am."

"Phoebe, my love, your guest is here," Freya announced.

With the fireplace warming her backside, Phoebe stood in a burgundy frock, wearing a necklace and heart-shaped earrings he recognized immediately as belonging to Maria Monteleone. Hugh stood beside her and gave a nervous grin. He frowned when he noted the roses.

"Miss Phoebe, these are for you."

She was in front of him in a flash, her pink nose buried in the velvet petals. The color reflected in her face and made it seem golden. The tiny earrings on charm hooks sizzled to the rhythm of her heartbeat.

She was nervous too.

"Thank you. And here it should be I presenting you a gift, not the other way around. But you are a true hero, aren't you, Lionel? Never seeking anything for himself."

Phoebe's father entered behind him and gave him a slap on the back. "If thanks are being had, please allow me to join the receiving line. You have done this family a great service, and for that we are eternally in your debt."

"I wasn't acting alone. Hugh also—" he began.

"Nonsense," Hugh objected. "You were the one who took notice and disposed of the garbage. All I did was return her to the safety of her family."

Phoebe had placed the flowers in a crystal vase, spreading and tending to them like Maria used to arrange her flowers. Lionel closed his eyes for a second and willed the past to leave him.

Phoebe stood so close to him that the muscles in his thighs began to expand, not to mention another body part that was complaining about being restricted. She began addressing her parents.

"I have something to share." Her hands were clasped inside themselves at her waist as if she was giving a music recital.

The brothers shared the warning gaze that sent

both their blood pressures rising and widened their eyes. Hugh looked like he was about to pass out, but very slightly shrugged, telling Lionel he had no idea what was to come.

"I was resistant to it at first," Phoebe continued. "But I've decided to make a change to my security detail. I've taken the trouble to consult Marcus on this just this morning."

Lionel swallowed. Hard. He widened his stance.

"Hugh and I have discussed this as well."

This brought a scowl to Hugh's brows and lips. He avoided Lionel's eyes.

"With Marcus and Hugh's permission, I've decided to switch my detail. I'm inviting Lionel to become my personal protector."

She could not know how much pain he was in. He wanted to shake her as he had last night at the bungalow, to make her come to her senses. In no way was this a safe thing to do.

As she smiled up at him, she took his hand. He took a step back. She giggled softly and grabbed his hand again.

"My mother has advised me it would be prudent to take a husband, until such time as I have found my fated mate," she whispered, lying through her teeth and making him want to put a paw over her mouth to stop her. But he was unable to say or do anything. Her fingers entwined with his in an intimate familiarity that was dangerous to both of them.

"Lionel, if you will allow my request, I am asking you to become my husband until that day comes. To protect me and act on my behalf, not as a paid employee, but as a husband would care for his wife."

This isn't wise, he found himself messaging her, though he knew she couldn't hear him. There was no way that the two species could hear each other.

But will you do it? came her answer. It completely immobilized him.

He looked at the little group, watching the way her chest heaved, breaking free from the low-cut frock she wore. Her hand was moist, and from it came a soothing glow that soon traveled all over his body. Her father's mouth hung open. His eyes were difficult to read. But Freya had clasped her breast and was smiling, tears streaming down her cheeks.

"Well done, Daughter. And look how shy he is. He is the perfect choice."

Lionel could tell Hugh was calculating and re-calculating in his head all the possible scenarios as if he'd arrived at the party late.

"Do you always make your ladies wait, Lionel?" Phoebe purred, pushing the envelope into dangerous territory.

"My ladies? I-I have never been asked to perform this task."

She'd stepped so close that now he could feel the heat of her body. Phoebe was hanging on every word.

"A husband? In name only, of course," Lionel continued.

"Yes, of course!" Salvatore Dominichelli blurted out nervously. "Phoebe is to remain virgin. There will be no consummation of this marriage. You have that correct, my man."

But her eyes challenged him as he saw the battle lines being drawn. He was torn between being the person her parents thought he was, the person Marcus and Paolo and the whole Monteleone clan thought he was, and the male she was becoming to know. The man who was feeding and tending a growing fate that would certainly complicate all their lives. And yet, he found strength in her face.

He suddenly didn't want to share her with the rest of the world.

Her blush told him he'd not been smart and had let his thoughts roam freely between them.

Is this a mistake, dear Phoebe?

All I want to know—and I won't ever be able to sleep

again until I do—is, will you do it?

He knew there was only one answer, God help him. He decided it would be good form to call up the God of mortals for extra strength. He went down on one knee.

"With God's help, I will serve you faithfully, will honor your womanhood, and protect you from harm. And I'll perform any and all the tasks that you require with a willing heart."

Out of the corner of his eye, he could see that even Hugh was calling on the God of mortals. His brother closed his eyes, bowed his head, and crossed himself, even though there was no one now who could save them.

Chapter 12

PLANS BEGAN WITHIN hours after it was confirmed by her father that, indeed, Marcus and the rest of his family had approved of the choice to take Lionel as her husband. Most of her friends and family were delighted. Those of the household staff were guarded and shared a level of enthusiasm that seemed tepid at best. Phoebe believed it to be because they still worried for her safety and expected she'd save herself and everyone around her by taking to the turning soon and *then* marry.

The subject had been brought up several times by her mother, and on each occasion, she fended off the arguments with the same resolve she'd had the day she made her decision.

"*After*, Mother. After some time, if I feel a calling to that part of my life, I will do so. In the meantime, could you just tolerate a mere mortal in your household for a bit longer?"

Freya always broke down and agreed with her each time they had the discussion. Phoebe was careful to thank her mother and her father and especially the household staff, on whom the burden of cooking, cleaning and protecting her mortal world fell. It was a world closer to them than that of her parents.

She decided to celebrate her new engagement at her dance studio, where she and Samuel had been learning ballroom and jazz couples dancing. She wanted to bring Lionel as her special guest of honor, but he refused. She had not seen him for two days after the announcement, and she was disappointed. But tonight would be his first night at the villa with them all.

"He's been preparing his things for the move tonight, Phoebe. I've helped Samuel take a room downstairs by the kitchen, since you are now an engaged young woman. Lionel will be here later on. You'll see. My duties are complete, and it's *adios* soon."

"I shall miss you, Huge."

He gave her a careful hug. "We've enjoyed our brief tryst, madam. Haven't we?" he said with a deep bow. He zipped his lips. "It will be our secret."

She was filled with giggles. "Have you ever been in love, Hugh?"

"I don't think there is love for most dark coven members. Not like what you feel, for instance. Most of us submit to a life of service, and there's meaning in that. Love is not a luxury we can afford."

"How sad," she said, touching his cheek.

"You have to stop touching me, lovely Phoebe. We can't be seen as too familiar. Only with your husband."

She thought the comment odd, but let it stand. "So fating would be how it works, then?" she pried.

Hugh turned his head from side to side as if he were helping the pieces of his brain to fit together, to give him a complete picture and a coherent answer. "I think that's mostly true. I'm sure the evil ones have just an animalistic blood lust. They'd eat their wives if it was necessary. Perhaps their children as well."

He shook all over.

"Would it be odd if a dark vamp did fall in love? Or felt the fating?"

"Ah, how clever of you." Hugh ticked his finger at her face. "I'm not going to willingly fall into that silver trap. You'll have to ask him yourself."

"Ask whom?" came the voice of Lionel behind her.

Phoebe ran to Lionel's arms, hitching skirts and wrapping her legs around his hips.

You shouldn't be doing this, Phoebe.

She noted the gruffness in his tone and met it with defiance of her own.

Stop me.

The picture he sent her made her drop to her knees, panting. In the vision, he'd removed her petticoats, slid down her panties, turned her over his knees, and was slapping her bare bottom so hard there were red welts the size of his enormous hands on each cheek.

She pulled herself up and frowned like a spoiled child, rubbing her backside.

"Ow."

Lionel sighed and faced the ceiling. Hugh was nearly doubling over with laughter. "Promise me, brother, you will take your fake honeymoon in a screened and protective space. I don't want to see any of it or know anything about it."

"There will be no honeymoon, Brother. She takes liberties at her home she will regret doing some day." Facing her, he repeated himself. "You should not get comfortable with these games, Phoebe. It's dangerous."

"See? I told you exactly the same," added Hugh.

"Very well." Vowing to get even, she demanded, "When you finish getting situated, there are a few items that require your attention."

Lionel turned his head, but she'd masked everything she could. "I'll be upstairs when you feel in the mood to serve."

As she left the room, she brushed against his thigh

with one of her own. When the electricity sparked the inside of her entire right leg, she hitched her breath and gave him a subtle moan.

All she heard at her back was some swearing. She thought Italian was much more pleasing to the ear, told him so telepathically, giggling all the way to the top of the second-floor landing and her bedroom beyond.

She heard cars on the driveway and then happy voices of her brothers returning with her parents. Phoebe ran to overlook downstairs and waved at Rodrigo and Santos. Their return had been delayed due to an emergency at the camp.

Little Santos was only eight and rattled stories to his mother in Italian. Rodrigo stood tall, then ran up to his sister.

"You were missed, Brother," she said as she hugged his bony frame.

His handsome face was partially covered by hair that had grown too long.

"Look at this!" she said, extending his curls out five inches from the sides of his head.

"Mama has already told me I'm to report to cook so I'm not mistaken for one of the coven ruffians." He pondered his well-worn canvas slip-ons. "They came, you know."

"I heard. Did they take anyone?"

He sadly nodded. "Two boys from families in Washington State who had apparently gotten lost in the forest. They found the bloody tracking devices stuffed in their backpacks with their cell phones."

The realities of being mortal were growing heavier with each passing week. Phoebe knew the wedding would be a welcome distraction for the entire Tuscan clans, as well as others from abroad.

"You heard my news, then?"

"Phoebe, I can't believe it. But a dark lord? How could you agree to obey and be companion to anyone but a Golden?"

"You see any eligible Goldens who want me?"

"He *wants* you? They are *allowing* you to do this?"

"No, silly. It's a marriage for protection and convenience. He's allowed certain liberties he wouldn't have as an employee. But the marriage is still for my protection. That's all you have to know."

"I couldn't do it, Phoebe. I just couldn't."

She pulled him to her again and, stroking the top of his head, whispered, "You're only fifteen, Rodrigo. Wait until you turn nineteen. You'll see things differently. Trust me on that."

She followed his skipping form upstairs to the third floor where her parents had their bedchamber. When she peered below, Lionel had just started the ascent with a cardboard box filled with several items. She waited until he passed her on the way to the room across from hers. He stopped in the hallway beyond, turned, and asked for directions. She pointed to the right.

At his doorway, she watched his massive back and upper arms from behind as he bent over the box laid tenderly on the bed, pulling several things out. She knew he sensed her.

"I'm supposed to be keeping an eye on you, not the other way around," he mumbled to his box.

"I find you fun to watch."

"Fun? What is that?" he said, holding an electronic piece of equipment with the cord dangling.

"The opposite of obligation. A freebie."

He had his room set up in less than five minutes.

"You always travel light?" she asked.

He stoked the fireplace with several new pieces of split oak. He washed his hands and then laid his canvas satchel next to the sink. He slowly approached with his head bowed. "I have very few things in this world that I care about. I require little in the way of comforts. I don't like jewelry or adornments. I am a simple man, Phoebe. You'll learn that about me in time."

"Am I—?" She was going to touch his cheek again, but he caught her wrist in mid-air.

"You make it difficult. Please, let me get my bearings first. My primary job is to keep you safe. I can't do that if I don't concentrate."

Her eyes teared up. Perhaps she'd been wrong, and what she was feeling wasn't matched on his side. Or maybe it was her mortality that caused her to be needy. He was warning her, and all she wanted to do was run into the danger of his arms.

It took courage to turn away from him and walk toward her doorway without looking back, until she heard the warm whisky of his voice.

"But the answer to your question, dear Phoebe, is yes. You are one of the things that I care about, a dangerous and pleasurable joy."

When she looked over her shoulder he didn't hide the deep studying perusal, drinking in every contour and feature of her body as if it was the last time he'd see her.

There. You feel how I want you, see you, Phoebe? Is it enough for now?

She knew he was hoping for a de-escalation between them, but her heart wouldn't let that happen. She dropped her arms by her sides.

It is not enough, Lionel. It will never be enough for me.

He reacted like he'd been slapped. He gulped in air and squeezed his hands into fists. She knew he was at the same edge she was, and it took her breath away.

They heard her mother and father were making their way upstairs. She waited for him to break eye contact first, and then swung herself over to the landing, embraced her mother, and kissed her good night. Her parents retired up the stairs, holding hands. Her mother was babbling about something she'd seen today at the market and was not paying attention to her, or to the dark man at her back whose eyes Phoebe could feel, whose hot breath warmed her from ten feet away where he stood at his own doorway, ready to fall into Hell with her, or anything else she might command.

Chapter 13

FEELING HER THOUGHTS was like watching a woman undress behind a frosted glass curtain. Occasionally, he'd catch a tinge of red or a fold of flesh with a charcoal grey shadow separating a smooth surface from a mysterious cavern.

The scent of her arousal seared his nostrils and made him bite his own tongue. He licked his lips and extended his hand so that his fingertips rested on the white flesh of her delicate shoulder. Pinching an errant curl from the back of her neck, he tucked it into the crystal-studded clip clasped there. His palm widened as he traveled the arch of her neck from the top of her blouse until his fingers dove into her hairline.

Phoebe leaned her head back, and he angled forward where he could place his cheek against hers. He inhaled her perfume, dabbed beneath her ear in the fine, delicate hairs. His lips parted as he ran his tongue along the jugular vein and felt the movement of attracted tissue below the surface.

She grabbed his hand and placed it to her breast, mating with his fingers and squeezing her flesh.

"I have never tasted anything so exquisite, Phoebe."

She slid in his arms to press her gentle body against his, pressing her mounds of flesh against his knotted nipples reaching out to her through the cotton of his shirt.

"I have need, Lionel. I can't think."

He held her head, his hands sliding to the graceful arch of her neck to clutch and pull her face to him.

"It is wrong, Phoebe. You know this is wrong." He marveled in the smooth marble of her skin, planting little kisses and hearing his love purring in her ear.

Having charmed her, he was going to pull away and flee to the safety of a locked oak door, but she lowered her chin, placed her fingers at his lips, and whispered, "Then kiss me like an appropriate arranged marriage partner would. Teach me how to be obedient to your will, my future consort, so that I can bloom alongside of you and give you comfort as a good wife should."

The prospect of teaching her about sex, being her first experience, patterning kisses over her body with the ancient mating knowledge, and filling her every orifice with his seed brought down his canines. As their lips met, she opened to him, sucking his tongue deep inside the warm cavern of her mouth. He repeated the kiss, curling to cover her tongue, caressing it under his sharp incisor and pricking the surface to taste her sweet elixir.

Her fingers covered his lips, her hot breath and mouth feeding from him. He clipped his own tongue and spread his blood over her teeth and gums, which made her shudder.

"Too much?" he whispered, running his fingers over the blue vein in her neck, admiring it like the wonder that was her body.

"No. Never too much. I. Need. This." She grabbed his head, deepening her kiss until he could barely breathe.

She pulled him backwards into her room and closed the door behind him. Then she began to disrobe.

"No."

She didn't pay attention and removed her blouse and a lacy undergarment.

"No, Phoebe. I won't be able to stop. We cannot do this."

Her fingers gripped the fabric of his shirt and jerked, popping the buttons all over the floor.

"Phoebe, your desire for me is flattering, but it's dangerous."

"Then do what you can. Do everything you can. Everything a husband is legally required and commanded to do. Serve me, Lionel. Make me whole. Change me forever."

He was losing the will to think. If he did not figure out something and quick, they'd not live to have another encounter.

He lifted her, draping her gently over her bed. By the light of the fireplace, he watched her peach body wracked with need. Her bare breasts stood in stiff peaks, her nipples bright red and bursting with the blood he'd summoned in her body. Seeing the power he had over her emboldened him further. His cock ardently sought redemption, but he denied himself, instead pulling up her skirts and exposing her sex to him.

He slid to the bed with his knees bent, supporting her buttocks in his lap, steadying her hips in an angle for his hungry tongue. He licked the gash between her legs, rubbing his sharp canines over her little bud, nicking it.

Her eyes flew open, and her hands clutched his thighs. Even through his trousers, she'd drawn blood. Her petals fell back on themselves as he pressed his thumb into her opening, then pinched and bled her nub, bringing the blood of her sex to his mouth.

"Yes. Taste me, Lionel."

He bent down, curling his tongue, before sliding it in and around the fleshy plug that held her virginity safely in place. He sucked at the young girl she was, begging her to become his woman with every stroke lovingly delivered.

He righted himself slowly, noticing the pain and satisfaction crossing her face and her desperate need for more. He considered the gray area in which he tread. Pleasuring her orally, he could make her come for him over and over again. Of that he was certain. He could fill her body with such exquisite pleasure she'd never want to be without him. He could give her all that.

But he could not give her the blood bite ritual that would forever alter her trajectory and rob her of her mortal life. He could lead her up to the precipice and then let her fall back into his arms over and over again until she had no strength left, until there was no breath in her body. She was not Maria. She was the woman Maria primed him for, the one he'd waited centuries to claim as his own.

But he'd have to wait a bit longer. He had no right to claim her fully. Not yet.

"Taste me," she moaned.

With hot tears in his eyes, he cried for the fourth

time. He licked the delicate, engorged lips of her sex, applied his spittle to the soft bowl between those golden folds and the top of her thigh, then bit deep and hard, robbing her of her blood, but not her virginity nor her mortal life. As her warm elixir traveled over his tongue and down his throat, everything became very clear.

They were indeed a fated pair, but they'd have to wait to assuage what he really needed most, and until he got permission, he'd have to remain unsatisfied.

Someday, he'd claim her for all eternity, for his own.

And nothing would be able to stop him.

Chapter 14

PHOEBE AWOKE ALONE, the sheets of her bed twisted and torn from the mattress. The taste of his sweet kisses still lingered in her mouth. She inhaled, stretching, feeling the power of the fire growing in her soul. She was going to find it difficult to spend the many daylight hours until they could physically be together again.

Selena arrived and put her hand to her mouth at the shocking sight of her ravished bed.

"Miss Phoebe. You had a difficult night?"

Phoebe rolled her head slowly in a careful circle, allowing her hair to hang and cover her laughing face. "Dreams. I had so many wild dreams."

"Your illness has returned then? Are you with fever again?" The young woman felt her forehead and shook her head, no. "Your stomach?" The attendant began to lift her nightgown, and Phoebe pressed it back down.

She didn't even remember putting on the gown, or what time it was when Lionel left her bed. Her petticoats and frock were thrown in a bundle in the corner.

Her bed was re-made, and she was ushered to the shower. "Your mother is waiting for you downstairs. Your future husband has locked himself in his room, but Samuel is awake and taking breakfast with your brothers."

"Thank you. I'll be down shortly."

The soapy bubbles were soothing, until she felt the dull ache at the top of her leg next to her sex. Her fingers traveled over two swollen bumps, once deep puncture wounds now healed but still evident. Her fingers came back without blood. She pressed the delicate tissue, and the pain made her cry out.

She quickly washed her hair, combing it out with the rare oil her father had brought back from one of his visits to North Africa. Her favorite pair of sloppy jeans slipped easily up to her hips and didn't disturb her wounds.

With her light pink lipstick applied to cover the raw red color her lips had become, she tied her hair back in a ponytail, and danced her way downstairs barefoot.

Her brothers were eating waffles and orange juice, as was Samuel, who sat across from them. She joined her family and took a fresh-squeezed glass for herself. Her parents sipped their daily cappuccino and shared a handful of grapes.

Freya was studying her carefully, her eyes boring into her flesh. Phoebe pretended not to notice by changing the subject.

"Samuel, tonight is the dance celebration. Perhaps we could go over to the hall and practice before nightfall?"

"Nothing would please me more," he said with a smile and toasted her with his orange juice.

Salvatore Dominichelli studied a paper in German, one of seven he read each day. Phoebe and her mother's eyes finally met. "Mother, would you like to attend the party this evening?"

"No. Our dancing days are over for right now. But we are going to the Monteleones', to listen to some new recordings Marcus has obtained. Very old and very rare." She lowered her lashes and smiled to her cappuccino. "And I'm going to discuss some arrangements for the wedding with Anne."

Of course, Phoebe thought. Lionel was not a man of means, and he only had bachelor brothers without wives, so there was no one on his side to help with the preparations.

"He likes things simple. Not fancy or ornate."

"Well then," she cleared her throat and returned with, "When he finds a fated female and has daughters of his own, he will understand that the groom has very little say about it. Everything is about the bride."

Samuel gave a puzzled expression, but her brothers kept eating.

PHOEBE AND SAMUEL rode their bicycles over to the studio. A car with two additional protectors followed a distance behind. The fall colors were ripe with oranges and deep burgundy, leaves skittling over the narrow cobblestoned streets.

The dance hall had been an assembly hall during World War II, a place for political speeches and protests, even some bloodshed, or so she was told. Her father confided to her about the olive oil and money he donated to the Italian armies, especially when they returned from losing campaigns. The family had considered moving to the States, but Salvatore was certain the winery and olive groves would be confiscated and never returned to them. They stayed to defend their lands, while appearing to defend the armies of their country and whatever politician they could befriend and trust.

But now the wooden building had been renovated and painted a soft peach. The wood floors inside were sanded and re-finished, making them perfect for dancing. The huge windows let in the most beautiful sunlight by day, showing full moon and stars at night.

A ballet class currently practiced, with youngsters of preschool age, dressed in pink tutus, taught by a skinny nun in a black modern habit. She and Samuel sat quietly and watched their attempts at running, leaping, and assuming various positions. The sister's exacting fingers, tried to make them do what their little limbs could not yet achieve.

The pianist was also the woman who occasionally drove several of the parish priests on their errands. She was a full-time resident at the Catholic school Phoebe had attended.

At last, she smiled in their direction, collected her music, waddled across the floor in lace-up shoes that squeaked. The bevy of young dancers disappeared like petals in the wind as their parents stopped by to pick them up.

Samuel took her hand and pulled her around the dance floor. She threw her head back and allowed the centrifugal force to pull her body, making it feel like she was flying. He broke his hold to turn on the music, and they cavorted back and forth in an Argentinian Tango. He held her close, then pushed her hip away with the palm of his other hand until she ran out of tether and came back to him. He spun her, slid on his knees to her feet, and even worked a cartwheel into the routine.

Phoebe was filled with delight.

"Where did you learn this?"

"I watch television, but my mother had always wanted me to be a dancer," he said, breathing heavily. "She took me everywhere to live shows. I loved them."

"But I can see you took it up. You're a natural."

"Never took lessons until recently, with you. But gymnastics was my gig. And then there was soccer—football as you call it here."

She followed his lead through several other sets and knew that, had she never met Lionel, she could convince herself to want to spend time with a man like this. He was handsome, athletic, and he liked to move and to laugh. He enjoyed exploring, and he smiled often. Life would be uncomplicated with someone like him.

But there would be no passion, no fire. No danger. She wanted to be stalked, hunted, and claimed. If she closed her eyes, she could imagine she was dancing in Lionel's arms.

As the next piece came on, Phoebe recognized the rhythm of a waltz. She assumed her square box arms position and allowed him to glide her across the floor, twirling, leaning back as she did so.

The two American protectors from the car showed

up in the doorway.

Samuel shrugged. "I think this means we have to go home."

THE AFTERNOON HOURS dragged on. She attempted to read a book. Then she took a nap by the fireplace downstairs. Samuel studied some maps, then grabbed his computer to order several items online. He called one of the other team members who were readying a trip back to California with Marcus and Paolo and the family.

Phoebe's mother and father left with her brothers for the evening with the Monteleones as the sun was setting. Her heart began to race the deeper blue it got outside, until she heard the distinctive turn of the lock and the heavy iron hinges squeak, indicating Lionel was now awake.

"He's up," she whispered to Samuel. "I'm going to try one more time to get him to come with us."

"Good luck with that. I'm going to shower, so I'll be ready whenever you are."

"Thank you for today. I had a wonderful time."

"Me too." He embraced her, giving her a quick kiss on her cheek.

Phoebe felt the hot eyes of her future husband burning a hole in the back of her neck and what sounded like a growl. She was not surprised to see Lionel standing at the foot of the stairway with his hands made into fists.

"Oh, I'm glad you're awake." She walked carefully towards him, slightly embarrassed by the fantasies dancing in her head she was trying desperately to mask. "Remember about the dance at the hall, Lionel? Samuel and I are going to go this evening. I know you've said no before, but could you please find it in your heart to accompany me—us?"

Samuel was motionless, waiting for Lionel's response.

"How long?" he asked.

Samuel spoke first before Phoebe could. "Not long. An hour, two at the most. She'd like to show you the routines we've worked out."

She heard his soft growl again.

Fingering a buttonhole in his shirt, she whispered, "And I wanted to formally introduce you to the other couples. It's not a large crowd. Why don't you come? I think you'd like it."

Please, Lionel. I would like you there, and I also think it would be smart.

"Okay, but I have no other help tonight, and your parents are gone. Hugh is with Jeb."

"Thank you." Phoebe turned to Samuel. "Go, off

with you. Get your shower in, quick!" She clapped her hands, and Samuel shot to the back of the kitchen and disappeared.

She returned to the buttonhole, but he caught her hand before she could slither her errant finger through to touch him.

Phoebe closed her eyes and angled her mouth up towards him. "Give me one of those appropriate, arranged marriage kisses that makes me loose my mind." Her lips created a generous pucker for effect.

He covered her mouth and gave her a taste of his blood, which sent an electric shot down her spine that made her tingle all over.

"You must promise me you'll be careful tonight," he whispered, stroking her cheek with the back of his hand.

"At the dance?"

"Yes, of course, at the dance. Be aware of everything. I don't know these people."

"But I do. Some of them are my turned cousins."

"All the more reason to be careful. No messages, Phoebe. We cannot take any chances we could be overheard."

"I'll try."

He gripped her arm and pulled it harshly to his side. "No. You won't *try*. You will behave."

"I promise I won't make a fool out of either one of us. I'll be your most compliant future wife. I'll do anything you ask me to do, Lionel. Anything."

IT WAS DELICIOUS being next to him in the back seat as Samuel drove her mother's car to the dance hall. She matched the rhythm of his breathing until he whispered, "Stop it."

Dancers had already taken their spots on the floor while several young women set out cookies and a Sangria-like punch based on an old, mulled wine recipe. She presented a cup to Lionel, and he declined.

She finished the warm liquid just in time for a young man to ask her to dance. He was new to the group, an American university student, he said. He held her loosely, not forcing himself at her while they waltzed. Every time he turned her, she saw Lionel's measured stare, noticing everything around her.

Samuel cut in, and they danced their West Coast Swing routine. One time during the dance, she swung close, barely grazing against Lionel's chest, and heard Lionel growl again. She tossed her head from side to side, rocked her hips to the rhythm of the lively music, and spun beneath Samuel's guidance.

They both clapped, and she scanned the room. Lionel had retreated to a dark corner until a woman dressed in a red poodle skirt pulled up a chair, and sat too close. He backed up discretely, but the woman leaned toward him, talking to him with her chin placed into the palm of her hand, her elbow on the table.

Phoebe decided to join the pair until a firm arm grabbed her around the waist and spun her tight against his muscled frame. Next to her cousin Daniel stood another newcomer. She smelled the distinctive vape of a dark vamp. She shot a worried look at Daniel as the dark vamp spoke.

"My lucky day. The legendary virgin Golden daughter without her protectors." His smile was disingenuous. Phoebe didn't trust him.

Daniel was trying to separate the two of them, but the vamp was much stronger.

"Get off me, boy. When you turn, you will become a man. This beauty desires a real man, don't you, dear Phoebe?"

She was shocked he knew her name, which again indicated Daniel had not been discrete with their family information. The newcomer squeezed her waist between his thumb and fingers, as if he was going to crush her ribs.

In a flutter of wind and dark cloth, Lionel was there. He'd inserted himself hard against the dark vamp, towering above him by several inches as he stepped on the man's foot. Phoebe could hear the crunch of bone and noted the slight sweat forming at the forehead of the newcomer, but he did not scream.

"You have an impending appointment with a physician and a cast maker, my young traveler. You are not welcome here." Lionel took back his foot and scanned the crowd.

"He came with me. We came alone," stuttered Daniel.

"He's my cousin. Daniel," Phoebe hurried.

"You make unwise choices, young Daniel."

"Who—?" Her cousin pointed to Lionel as a crowd began to form around the little circle.

Phoebe inhaled and took Lionel's hand. "He is my husband-to-be, Daniel. This was to be the night I was going to introduce you all to him."

Frowns turned into smiles as the room erupted in spontaneous clapping. Out of the corner of her eye, she noticed the dark guest limp toward the doorway and slither away into the night. She looked up at Lionel, who was following the same line of sight.

Lionel was asked to dance, and he declined repeatedly. Instead, he stood in the middle of the floor, watching Phoebe take partner after partner. He was never more than a handful of feet from her side, which became quite the topic of whispers and tittering laughter. But he remained motionless except for the small steps he needed to take to get closer to her. Occasionally, he glanced out the windows and doorway, but for most of the remaining minutes, he was transfixed watching her and every movement she made.

The trip home was silent. Samuel gave up making small talk and resigned himself to being just the driver.

Inside the kitchen, she gave the young protector a hug and then watched him retire to his room, closing the door behind.

Lionel had checked the doors and windows. She knew they were now alone. What she'd been dreaming of all day was suddenly here.

"Lionel, thank you. I—"

But his lips covered her mouth, then hoisted her in his arms and traced upstairs to his bedroom. The strong scent of his sleep still drifted past her, making her ears buzz and her heart pound. At his back she saw the dark carved four-poster bed that had been in her family for generations.

"Your parents will return soon," he whispered to her. His fingers slipped her blouse over her shoulder, and he kissed her there. Her lips grazed past his rough cheek. She pressed her forehead to the side of his face.

"What are we to do? This is driving me mad."

"I can relieve the pressure, give us both a temporary reprieve until we are assured of being alone again, but there is a limit to my will power, and if I should fail—"

She sucked his lower lip, pressing her mound to his groin. "Then you will take me with you to Hell and back. I want an unbridled kiss with your full heart."

He looked upon her in the firelight. "I promised your mother. I will not break that vow, but understand if I could, I'd fill you with my seed, and I'd demand every ounce of your soul."

"When? Lionel, when? Will it ever happen?"

"On my life, I will find a way to love you to eternity."

"And if I remain human?"

"Eternity for me is the same whether you are turned or human, sweet Phoebe. I've done it once. But this will be the last time."

"Take my wrist and give me yours."

He sliced a thin line of red across his left wrist and placed it to her lips. She drew hard, attempting to increase the size of the wound.

"No. There is much to teach you first. Just enough to start the burn in your belly. Do you feel it? If we are fated, you will burn. And you will bleed."

"I already have, Lionel." She lapped the remaining

lifeblood from her lips. "Now, take from me."

She held out her wrist, but he fell to his knees, smoothing both hands up her leg beneath her skirts, and discovered she'd worn no panties. He spread her thighs, then dipped his head beneath the layers of petticoat fabric, laving her swollen bud and drawing her lips under the tip of his canine. He nipped her, which made her shiver from the surprise and the pleasure of it. His thick tongue pressed against the little bumps where he'd wounded her last night. He inhaled and breached her flesh again.

She knew the more their blood mixed, the more she'd demand from him. She hoped they'd create a solution to their mating issue before it was too late.

Minutes later, he was carrying her to her own bed.

This will have to be enough for tonight, my bride.

It will never be enough for me, she told him just before she fell into a deep sleep.

Chapter 15

MARCUS WELCOMED LIONEL to the library for the requested audience.

"What brings you to my home, Lionel? Everything progressing with your plans for the wedding? Any second thoughts or regrets?"

"No, sir. I am good with my decision."

"And my cousin Phoebe, is she doing any better with the manners?"

Lionel smiled to the floor. "That's going to always be a problem."

Marcus laughed. He handed Lionel a tumbler containing legendary whiskey from his extensive collection. The drink was smooth and helped to settle his nerves.

"Then is that why you've come?"

"I fear I need marital advice," Lionel blurted out before he lost his courage altogether.

Marcus uncrossed his legs, set his drink down, and leaned forward in his leather rocker. "You surprise me.

Isn't this soon to have marital discord? The wedding is tomorrow."

"She desires that I—do things to her of a sexual nature. I am her husband, but in name only. I understand this. But she is bending the boundaries—and I don't mean to blame her for this, as I feel a strong attraction myself. But I wouldn't be the man you can count on if I didn't inform you of this."

There. It was said. He'd tossed all day and most of his waking time the night before rehearsing over and over what he wanted to tell Marcus.

"I see."

Lionel finished his drink but was not offered another. He didn't want to impose so set the empty goblet down. He'd made another miscalculation. Perhaps this wasn't news Marcus could receive.

"Is it like a fating, then?"

"Well, it couldn't be, could it? I mean, all my life I've been told that's impossible between the species."

"But you feel something? The same as she?"

"I don't think so, no. Could it be that she has what mortals call love? Could it be a real love and not an animalistic fating? Perhaps something purer?"

Marcus paced across the heavily carpeted floor.

"I'm looking first for an explanation before I can decide what to do," Lionel admitted.

"You aren't considering calling everything off, are you?"

"Should I? Tell me honestly, Marcus."

"You would have shamed her. Does her family know of this?"

"We've not violated anything for which we should feel guilty. Perhaps stretched the boundaries a bit. I call it healthy experimentation."

"With a Golden female."

Lionel was disappointed to discover now he was feeling shame for his lack of restraint. "I have not penetrated her. She is and will always be virgin while I'm alive to protect her. No worries there. I haven't broken my vow to her family or to her."

"Who is responsible for instigating the advances?"

Lionel didn't want to answer, so he lied. "I guess that would be me."

Marcus began to laugh again. "Lionel, you are the last of the honest men on this planet. Are you sure a Golden is not in your bloodline?"

"I'm not understanding, sir."

"You just lied to me. I don't believe for a minute you forced her or glammed her or, in any way, began this relationship." He grabbed Lionel's goblet and headed for the minibar. "She's done to you what my mother couldn't bring herself to do."

He didn't think he'd heard Marcus correctly. Did Marcus know of his love for his mother?

"I've never spoken of my feelings for your mother. I assure you, Marcus, nothing inappropriate happened there. I knew my place then, and I know my place now."

"I've not told you everything I know, Lionel. I think both Paolo and I have noticed the chemistry between the two of you. I was not aware of the fondness you and my mother had for each other until I was told at a much older age. When I first saw the now-grown Phoebe, the first person I thought of was you and how it would affect you to meet her."

"Of course. I understand all this."

"But the distance between our species is of great interest to me. And I've done some research."

"I *knew* you'd found the book!" he said as he stood.

"Sit." Marcus handed him the goblet. "You and Paolo are the only people who know, other than Ann and Paolo's wife, Carabella, who led us to the book."

"The Book of Spawn."

"The very one."

He pressed a panel of walnut on the wall, revealing a safe. Marcus dialed the combination and unlocked the dark compartment. He removed a large, ragged book several inches thick and laid it on the table next to Lionel.

"It's an odd book. It doesn't read from front to back, but from the middle to the front, with another story from the middle to the back. It's written in multiple languages, and the passages contain riddles and clues to other passages so that it's nearly impossible to follow sequentially. I've merely scratched the surface, and it reveals more questions than it does answers."

"May I?"

Marcus nodded, allowing Lionel to pick up the book and examine the front and back covers. The canvas was worn along the spine; gold lettering was partially rubbed off. As Lionel held it, he felt a faint heartbeat coming from the pages inside. He looked up at his employer.

"You feel it too?"

Lionel nodded.

"Then this confirms what I'd suspected all along. There is a connection between our families. Your story, our story, stories that are not yet lived are written in this book, I think."

"Why would the evil ones want such a storybook? If it isn't written for them, why value it so highly, or is it just because it's of value to you that they want to possess it?"

"It explains the origins of our species. Ours, yours, and human mortals."

Lionel was confused.

"We share a common bloodline, Lionel. We are branches of the same tree. The tree of life."

Lionel handed the book back to Marcus. "Put it away. I am not to be trusted with this relic. You must never let it leave your side."

Marcus placed the tome back in the safe, turned the knob, then closed the secret door. He dragged a chair so that he could sit knee-to-knee with his employee. Or was he now considered family?

"When I told you at the conclave that you were family, I'd gained this knowledge from the book. I don't know who I can trust. I may not be able to trust members of my own Golden clan. I may need someone who is seemingly on the outside, like you."

"I sensed the pirate had knowledge of our meeting already, Marcus. I told you so when I returned."

"Indeed. But I don't know who. One thing is certain. It isn't you, or Paolo."

"And I don't think it could be Hugh, or Jeb. Jeb was gone when the meeting took place, already the man's prisoner."

"Yes. But for the time being, only the three of us will know a very important secret. If I didn't trust you with the lives of my children, nieces, nephews, my wife, my siblings, and their wives and children, I would keep this from you."

"Keep what?"

"It tells of a people who lived for centuries, and as their culture evolved, they created rules and mores. Subsets of people. Some were satisfied, and some were bored with their lineage. Many no longer thought it was a higher form to live immortally."

"They had perfection, and they rejected it?" Lionel found this hard to believe.

"No, they didn't reject it. They *altered* it."

Lionel sat up straight and finished his drink. He examined the colorful chards cut into the crystal, sending tiny pieces of a rainbow onto the wall and ceiling above. "They created the separation of the species?"

"Yes."

"So who came first?"

"Think about it. They lived forever but wanted to make a finite choice, so they created the dark creatures of your line. To control the new breed, they imposed limitations, so they would be easier to track and to regulate."

"Go on."

"And then they created a species that would never

be immortal. Fearing these would take over the earth, they built into their DNA a failsafe date. They would die. They were stripped of their ability to choose between a mortal life and that of our lineage. The Goldens were the ones who messed it all up for everyone."

"They messed with the creation of the perfect being." The logic was undeniable and explained so many things which Lionel had pondered for years.

Marcus scooted his chair closer and grabbed Lionel's hand. "We are distant cousins. All of us. And what that means is there could be intermingling of the species. And perhaps what was done could be undone."

"What do we do with this information, Marcus?"

"For now, we keep it from everyone, especially the evil ones. They must never learn what we three now know. Until we are armed with some kind of way we can find a solution. For everyone."

Chapter 16

PHOEBE'S WEDDING DAY was beginning. Unlike most blushing brides, she could not see her husband until he emerged from his locked room. There would be no wedding in the sunshine with flower petals falling from baskets held by little angels.

But for a man who loved simple things, Lionel's request to be married in the chapel was an odd one. It was the chapel where Marcus had wed Anne, where he had first met his fated female in her mortal form, and first began his long journey to follow her, protect her, and eventually claim her for his own.

She was aware he'd spent some time in the chapel in quiet reflection last night, that he'd started to become interested in her stories about the family she was raised in.

Over the years, it had been said that the dark vamps had no soul, or were prone to evil, yet she had found in Lionel one of the most tender men she'd ever met. His depth of understanding of her kind wasn't as matched to her understanding of him. He dismissed his history as unimportant, and that surprised her.

So the evening wedding was to be a church service, with children's choirs and a chorus of nuns from the local school. There was to be a processional of accolades swinging incense like was done centuries ago. It was an ornate service, with lots of detail. Far from being simple, he had embraced this wedding as if a miracle were to be performed before their eyes.

He'd talked her into traveling back to California soon, so they could live on the Healdsburg Monteleone estate with Marcus and Anne. Phoebe was anxious to live where things were new and not centuries old. And although Lionel would never be able to enjoy it, she looked forward to the California sun.

For now, her mother and father were told none of their plans. The antique vestments were brought out, linens hundreds of years old and only worn on high holy days. Her dress was once worn by Marcus' mother. Her necklace complimented the intricate lace at her bodice. Lionel had insisted he place the heart-shaped earrings on her ears himself and told her he was ready to trace them some place private, so he could have her all to himself. He didn't believe in the superstition about seeing the bride before the wedding.

Nothing was going to dampen her desire for the

perfect wedding, or how she was going to demonstrate her love for this man.

The service moved her to tears. By candlelight, he removed her veil and tenderly tucked his fingers beneath her jawline, placing a blood-stained kiss there that she would remember the rest of her days.

The audience was so quiet. The mixture of mortals, dark, and Golden vamps dotted the pews and shed tears together, some with hands entwined.

As they made their exit, he lifted her like he'd done several times in secret, carried her down the aisle. She felt like she was the prize of his life.

As the weeks turned to Christmas, her mother stopped correcting her when she touched his lips in front of the family, and when she smiled at his strong embrace. The marriage between them was turning into something more than an arrangement, and everyone knew it.

She began to believe in miracles.

Afterword

CARMINE MONTELEONE WAITED at the little espresso stand and watched mortals rush children to school as well as scurry to their employers. Mixed in with them were a scattering of pigeons, harvesting crumbs along the cobblestone streets and walkways, dodging pedestrians and cars.

The traveler was larger than he'd imagined, and the gash running diagonally across his face was an unpleasant sight. He was unaccustomed to seeing disfigurement, especially on the face. But mortals could not help their lot in life. Their flesh did not heal fully, replenish itself, nor was it free from the aging process.

The rest of him looked healthy. Carmine would even say glowing. He'd been told of this mortal's appetites, which probably contributed to his robust build and sharp eyes. He was the most dangerous mortal he'd ever met.

"Espresso?" he asked, trying to appear casual.

"Nah."

As the young waitress arrived he ordered a Campari soda over ice. Carmine never understood the fascination with watered down sweet drinks, though this wasn't as sweet as some that mortals craved. The fruit didn't taste real, but then he was not a big fan of the food anyway. He preferred aged heavy spirits that took centuries to ripen in casks as old as he was. But he hid his second disgust of the day.

"I take it your trip was uneventful?" he asked the big man. That's when he noticed his deformed ear, like part of it had been bitten or torn off with teeth that definitely were not mortal.

"Delightful, as a matter of fact. You ever travel on those beautiful planes? They do everything for you except suck your cock. I slept like a baby."

Carmine nodded. He'd never ridden in a plane. When he was a child, before his turning, they hadn't been invented yet.

"What's it like for you?"

Carmine wasn't sure what the question was. "Excuse me?"

"Flying. Or are you lot all about tracing, moving across the globe in seconds or minutes without enjoying any of it? Not like you don't have the time to spare."

The elder Monteleone returned a brittle smile. "It

isn't the flying. It's putting my life in the hands of the mortal flying the plane."

"Ah." When his drink was served, he guzzled it halfway down, spilling several pinkish drops on his tunic. "Well, perhaps that will change. I can see your dark brethren becoming pilots."

Carmine could imagine the scene. Pilot and co-pilot who were dark coven vamps, taking turns harvesting the four hundred or so unlucky passengers. It would be messy, he thought.

"You could always trace," the traveler said.

"Not from a pressurized environment. I might turn up melded into a window or an engine blade."

"That's funny. I like your sense of humor, Monteleone. You think on your feet."

Carmine had been merely telling the truth.

"Have you found the girls?" the big man asked.

"Disappeared into thin air. No one has seen any of them."

"Well, there will be time enough for that. After. It will take years to extract my revenge once I do."

Carmine decided to change the subject because he wasn't liking the string of disgusting things he'd been imagining so early in the morning. He'd been in a good mood when he left his villa. Now he felt as wet and helpless as the pigeons at his feet who couldn't find enough food.

"So what's next, Salaman?"

"You get me the book."

"But like I've been telling you, I'm not sure where it is."

The mortal leaned across the table and was not smiling. "I've traveled a fair distance and foregone some more pleasurable pastimes to come here. I expect that you will fulfill your end of the bargain. Otherwise, we have nothing to discuss."

Carmine nearly peed his pants. Although Salaman's promise of riches was a motivating factor for him, his primary motive was to secure the safety of his family, especially his wife and three children and their offspring. He'd grown tired waiting for the Monteleone heads to come up with a foolproof plan to assure everyone's safety. And while most of his relatives were wealthy, his lineage had squandered their wealth, making poor investments. He'd married into his wife's money. So, even though he was a Monteleone, his wife controlled what money they had.

He had to beg for every Euro of spending money.

"I will find it," he said at last, his voice changing an octave.

"And tell me again why you are certain of this?" the traveler demanded.

"Because I've asked Marcus three times, and all three times, I'm sure he's lied to me. He tells me they are working on some leads but won't tell me what they are. He's an honest man, and honest men don't make very good liars."

"We agree on that. That's why I chose you."

Carmine squirmed in his seat, re-crossed his trousers, and took another sip of coffee. His hand shook as he brought the little white porcelain teacup down onto the saucer with a rattle.

Hoping to deflect another unpleasant image, Carmine blurted out, "Have you heard the news about the female you seek?"

Salaman finished his drink. His expression was a challenge. "Humor me."

Carmine was going to enjoy the next few seconds, which might be the only happy ones he'd ever have with this man again. He slowly emptied his little espresso cup and smiled.

"She's taken a husband." He savored the look of shock on the traveler's face.

"And she's—"

"Yes, yes. No fear there. It's a marriage of convenience. It is not a fating, and she's supposed to still be a virgin. She's married him for protection and nothing more, although there are rumors of—"

Salaman grabbed Carmine by the collar and yanked him across the table, oblivious to the passers-by, who shied away and whispered amongst themselves.

"Tell me the name of this unfortunate gentleman who is about to find himself disemboweled."

Carmine removed Salaman's hands like they were dirty rags, straightened up his jacket and shirt underneath, and sat tall. "You know this man."

"Who, dammit?" the traveler demanded, pounding the table and sending silverware to the sidewalk.

"Lionel Jett."

Watch for *Midnight Bite*, a full-length novel, Book 4 in the Golden Vampires of Tuscany Series, to be released in December 2019. Be sure to follow Sharon on Book Bub, Amazon and sign up for her newsletter so you won't miss this stunning new climax to the Golden Vampire saga.

BookBub: bookbub.com/authors/sharon-hamilton

Newsletter: authorsharonhamilton.com

About the Author

NYT and USA Today best-selling author Sharon Hamilton's award-winning Navy SEAL Brotherhood series have been a fan favorite from the day the first one was released. They've earned her the coveted Amazon author ranking of #1 in Romantic Suspense, Military Romance and Contemporary Romance categories, as well as in Gothic Romance for her Vampires of Tuscany and Guardian Angels. Her characters follow a sometimes rocky road to redemption through passion and true love.

Now that he's out of the Navy, Sharon can share with her readers that her son spent a decade as a Navy SEAL, and he's the inspiration for her books.

Her Golden Vampires of Tuscany are not like any vamps you've read about before, since they don't go to ground and can walk around in the full light of the sun.

Her Guardian Angels struggle with the human charges they are sent to save, often escaping their vanilla world of Heaven for the brief human one. You won't find any of these beings in any Sunday school class.

She lives in Sonoma County, California with her husband and her Doberman, Tucker. A lifelong organic gardener, when she's not writing, she's getting *verra verra* dirty in the mud, or wandering Farmers Markets looking for new Heirloom varieties of vegetables and flowers. She and her husband plan to cure their wanderlust (or make it worse) by traveling in their Diesel Class A Pusher, Romance Rider. Starting with this book, all her writing will be done on the road.

She loves hearing from her fans:
Sharonhamilton2001@gmail.com

Her website is:
sharonhamiltonauthor.com

Find out more about Sharon, her upcoming releases, appearances and news when you sign up for Sharon's newsletter.

Facebook:
facebook.com/SharonHamiltonAuthor

Twitter:
twitter.com/sharonlhamilton

Pinterest:

pinterest.com/AuthorSharonH

Amazon:

amazon.com/Sharon-Hamilton/e/B004FQQMAC

BookBub:

bookbub.com/authors/sharon-hamilton

Youtube:

youtube.com/channel/UCDInkxXFpXp_4Vnq08ZxM
BQ

Soundcloud:

soundcloud.com/sharon-hamilton-1

Sharon Hamilton's Rockin' Romance Readers:

facebook.com/groups/sealteamromance

Sharon Hamilton's Goodreads Group:

goodreads.com/group/show/199125-sharon-hamilton-
readers-group

Visit Sharon's Online Store:

sharon-hamilton-author.myshopify.com

Join Sharon's Review Teams:

eBook Reviews:

sharonhamiltonassistant@gmail.com

Audio Reviews:
sharonhamiltonassistant@gmail.com

Life is one fool thing after another.
Love is two fool things after each other.

Reviews

PRAISE FOR THE
GOLDEN VAMPIRES OF TUSCANY SERIES

"Well to say the least I was thoroughly surprise. I have read many Vampire books, from Ann Rice to Kym Grosso and few other Authors, so yes I do like Vampires, not the super scary ones from the old days, but the new ones are far more interesting far more human then one can remember. I found Honeymoon Bite a totally engrossing book, I was not able to put it down, page after page I found delight, love, understanding, well that is until the bad bad Vamp started being really bad. But seeing someone love another person so much that they would do anything to protect them, well that had me going, then well there was more and for a while I thought it was the end of a beautiful love story that spanned not only time but, spanned Italy and California. Won't divulge how it ended, but I did shed a few tears after screaming but Sharon Hamilton did not let me down, she took me on amazing trip that I loved, look forward to reading another Vampire book of hers."

"An excellent paranormal romance that was exciting, romantic, entertaining and very satisfying to read. It had me anticipating what would happen next many times over, so much so I could not put it down and even finished it up in a day. The vampires in this book were different from your average vampire, but I enjoy different variations and changes to the same old stuff. It made for a more unpredictable read and more adventurous to explore! Vampire lovers, any paranormal readers and even those who love the romance genre will enjoy Honeymoon Bite."

"This is the first non-Seal book of this author's I have read and I loved it. There is a cast-like hierarchy in this vampire community with humans at the very bottom and Golden vampires at the top. Lionel is a dark vampire who are servants of the Goldens. Phoebe is a Golden who has not decided if she will remain human or accept the turning to become a vampire. Either way she and Lionel can never be together since it is forbidden.

I enjoyed this story and I am looking forward to the next installment."

"A hauntingly romantic read. Old love lost and new love found. Family, heart, intrigue and vampires. Grabbed my attention and couldn't put down. Would definitely recommend."

PRAISE FOR THE
SEAL BROTHERHOOD SERIES

"Fans of Navy SEAL romance, I found a new author to feed your addiction. Finely written and loaded delicious with moments, Sharon Hamilton's storytelling satisfies like a thick bar of chocolate." —Marliss Melton, bestselling author of the *Team Twelve* Navy SEALs series

"Sharon Hamilton does an EXCELLENT job of fitting all the characters into a brotherhood of SEALS that may not be real but sure makes you feel that you have entered the circle and security of their world. The stories intertwine with each book before…and each book after and THAT is what makes Sharon Hamilton's SEAL Brotherhood Series so very interesting. You won't want to put down ANY of her books and they will keep you reading into the night when you should be sleeping. Start with this book…and you will not want to stop until you've read the whole series and then…you will be waiting for Sharon to write the next one." (5 Star Review)

"Kyle and Christy explode all over the pages in this first book, *[Accidental SEAL]*, in a whole new series of SEALs. If the twist and turns don't get your heart jumping, then maybe the suspense will. This is a must read for those that are looking for love and adventure with a little sloppy love thrown in for good measure." (5 Star Review)

PRAISE FOR THE
BAD BOYS OF SEAL TEAM 3 SERIES

"I love reading this series! Once you start these books, you can hardly put them down. The mix of romance and suspense keeps you turning the pages one right after another! Can't wait until the next book!" (5 Star Review)

"I love all of Sharon's Seal books, but *[SEAL's Code]* may just be her best to date. Danny and Luci's journey is filled with a wonderful insight into the Native American life. It is a love story that will fill you with warmth and contentment. You will enjoy Danny's journey to become a SEAL and his reasons for it. Good job Sharon!" (5 Star Review)

PRAISE FOR THE
BAND OF BACHELORS SERIES

"*[Lucas]* was the first book in the Band of Bachelors series and it was a phenomenal start. I loved how we got to see the other SEALs we all love and we got a look at Lucas and Marcy. They had an instant attraction, and their love was very intense. This book had it all, suspense, steamy romance, humor, everything you want in a riveting, outstanding read. I can't wait to read the next book in this series." (5 Star Review)

PRAISE FOR THE
TRUE BLUE SEALS SERIES

"Keep the tissues box nearby as you read *True Blue SEALs: Zak* by Sharon Hamilton. I imagine more than I wish to that the circumstances surrounding Zak and Amy are all too real for returning military personnel and their families. Ms. Hamilton has put us right in the middle of struggles and successes that these two high school sweethearts endure. I have read several of Sharon Hamilton's military romances but will say this is the most emotionally intense of the ones that I have read. This is a well-written, realistic story with authentic characters that will have you rooting for them and proud of those who serve to keep us safe. This is an author who writes amazing stories that you love and cry with the characters. Fans of Jessica Scott and Marliss Melton will want to add Sharon Hamilton to their list of realistic military romance writers." (5 Star Review)